Staying Down

Mike Stephens

Published by Mike Stephens, 2024.

STAYING DOWN

First edition. November 11, 2024.

Written by Mike Stephens.

In memory of Thomas Stanley 'Stan' Stephens.

In appreciation of my brother, Mark Stephens, for his friendship and unending support.

Acknowledgements

• • • •

To my niece, Hayley, for uncovering an old manuscript in my garage and urging me to publish it.

• • • •

And to Louise Nicholas without whose technical help the manuscript would never have left the garage.

CHAPTER ONE

The insipid light of dawn was beginning to creep past the edges of the crumpled curtains in David Rhys's bedroom. It was going to be a day to remember; the day on which they would shut the steelworks; the day when the hopes and jobs of the community of terraced streets would be lost; the day of the last of the dolomites.

-C'mon son, or you'll be late, shouted David's father from the foot of the narrow staircase.

Thomas Rhys had got a good fire going in the grate, even though it was mid-June, and had returned to his seat to drink a cup of strong tea and to smoke his first cigarette of the day. Early morning was the best time for him when he could read the paper and share a few words with Pat, his wife, before going on to the club where he was steward. Sometimes he stared into the fire and remembered his days underground, the back-breaking travelling to the coalface, his butties in the welfare club afterwards, and the sense of personal pride in being regarded by his fellow colliers as a good miner. But his old pit was now shut and abandoned, and the dust had long before then played havoc with his chest. So, Thomas Rhys had left the Welsh valley of his birth and had come here to the coast, to Cwmporth and its Riverside area, to earn a living as the steward of the Coronation Road Working Men's Club and Institute.

The family lived in tied accommodation - a grubby, crumbling terrace in Granall Street close to the River Effyl and the Sceptre Steelworks, which was sited on the opposite bank of the river. The only virtue of the steward's job was that the house adjoined the rear entrance to the club via a narrow enclosed alleyway and a yard, which contained the lock-up bottle shed. At least there was no longer any hard travelling to work, but the job was about the best that a worn-out fifty-four-year-old man with no transferable skills could expect to get.

-David mun! It's nearly five. Get a move on! Thomas Rhys shouted again but more loudly this time.

David recognized in his father's call that he had better not try his patience any longer and, reluctantly, he raised himself slowly out of bed. As he placed his bare feet on the cold lino' he saw in the half light the black pats scurrying off. They darted towards the safety of the holes in the skirting-board, their black shiny bodies marching across the uneven floor and their slender antennae slicing through the musty air. David watched the last cockroach disappear before he got up and went into the small bathroom to wash and shave. The mirror reflected a young man's face, which since it looked more thoughtful than most might have been taken for that of a twenty-five- or twenty-six-year-old. In fact, David was twenty-two and had lived most of his life in Cwm-porth. His parents' original home in Tredegar was known to him only in his father's stories and in his boyhood memories of visits to his nan before she went all funny and later, much later it seemed to a small boy, she died.

Now, before the mirror stood a tall and lean man, with an easy-going manner and a quiet confidence in his own abilities. David splashed cold water on his face and proceeded to scrape away the bristles with a blunt razor. Then he combed his thick black hair, and his blue eyes inspected the finished article in the mirror. He would do. Although his glance registered approval for what David considered to be a handsome appearance, behind the generous smile and the quick, agile body there was a slowly growing sadness, which sometimes made him distant and reserved. It was a sadness caused by living an endlessly grubby existence; by listening to the constant coughing of his father, which was made worse by the addictive supply of fags; and by watching the increased signs of worry and tiredness etched into his mother's face. Today David would go to the steelworks and complete his last shift, after which he supposed the grubbiness would become worse.

Thomas Rhys heard his son moving around upstairs and put the kettle on again to make a fresh pot of tea. Shortly, David came into the scullery and sat down by the fire. His father handed him a mug of thick sugary tea. Thomas Rhys had big hands and a powerful upper body, the product of many years working underground in cramped spaces hewing the coal from narrow seams. His face was thin and narrow but he also had a large, slightly bent, nose - the product of a motorcycle accident in his youth - and bushy eyebrows. He used plenty of Brylcreem on his black hair despite the fact that it was both receding and thinning. Most of all he had a reassuring smile, which he often bestowed on his son of whom he was immensely proud. The overall impression of Thomas Rhys was of a large and powerful man, but not brutish nor insensitive. Indeed, to David he had always been a strong yet gentle father, but now his bouts of coughing were becoming progressively worse and his health seemed ever more fragile.

-That's a good cup dad, said David as his father sat down opposite.

-Given any thoughts to what you'll do after today? asked Thomas in his quiet way.

-Naw. I'll go down the exchange tomorrow and see what's what. But round yere there'll not be much work when they shut the plant, replied David.

Thomas Rhys seemed to hesitate a moment. Then he put his cup on the fender and turned towards David.

-You can always help me out in the club, you know. I'll see you're okay for a few bob. It's up to you. See how you feel.

-Thanks dad, David said warmly. I'll see how I go on. You know I'm not too keen on a few of the members.

-Oh, they're not so bad, said Thomas with little conviction.

-Don't talk so far back dad, David replied with a broad smile, using one of his mother's favourite phrases.

His father gave a little chuckle.

-Well, you'd better be off to work and I'd better get another pot of tea on the go for your mam. She'll be up now in a minute.

David gathered up the small parcel of sandwiches his mother had made the night before. He said cheerio to his father and headed through the front room towards the door. As he put on his coat he felt a soft crunching under his foot; it was a black pat that had not made it to the safety of some cranny and that now lay on the carpet oozing a viscous white liquid from underneath its crushed shell. He noticed that the black pats hadn't touched any of the poison put down for them. David picked up the sagging remains and threw them into the street.

Granall Street at five thirty in the morning was quiet, and only a few fellow steelworkers could be seen walking along the long row of terraced houses. They would easily get to the Sceptre Works for clocking on by six, for although the plant was on the other side of the River Effyl a steel suspension bridge was only a few minutes walk from the top of Granall Street. Next to Granall Street was Ribley Street, both running parallel to the river and each locked into the same slow spiral towards decay and dereliction. Physically there was little to distinguish the two rows of terraces, but Ribley Street had the bigger reputation as a breeding ground for young thugs and for problem families - the kind of people the respectable working class look down on. It did not entirely deserve this reputation for there were plenty enough troublemakers who lived elsewhere in Riverside. Part of its disreputable image stemmed from the fact that Ribley Street was the closest to the river, and people liked to believe that in the Riverside area the nearer you lived to the open sewer, otherwise called the Effyl, the worse class of person you were.

David had not walked far from his own house when he passed by number 19 where he heard Old Man Morgan inside coming down the stairs, each step preceded by the thump of a heavy walking stick to steady his progress. At the top of the street David turned right into Dankley Alley, which ran east-west through Riverside and linked

Coronation Road to the dirt track directly bordering the river. Along Coronation Road there were more signs of life as steelmen on their way towards the bridge called into the papershop to buy their daily rag and ration of fags. Next to the shop stood the front entrance of the Coronation Road Working Men's Club and Institute, its sign still lit up from the night before. Reaching the junction of Coronation Road and Dock Road, David turned left and soon began to walk along the steep gradient of the ramp towards the suspension bridge. Within a hundred yards he had risen above the level of the chimney tops, many of them secreting grey wisps of smoke, and in front and to his left he could see the whole of Riverside.

It was an area of long terraced streets pressing up against small factories, jobbers yards, and scrap and repair firms, each employing a few hands. Most of these places depended on the steelworks for orders. Even the local power-station, just before Dock Rd, sent the majority of its electricity to the plant. A little way beyond the end of Ribley and Granall streets was the district's only park, known affectionately as 'Smelly Park' because it was right next to a glue works and to an old industrial chemical dump, called with somewhat less affection, 'The Brownhills'. But in Riverside nothing was very far from the Effyl, a wide, swift-flowing and deep channel bisecting Cwmporth.

Just to the right of the arching span of the bridge was the outflow for the cooling water used in the power-station. Two huge pipes were positioned under a wooden jetty, which had been used years ago as a landing stage for small ships, and at low tide when the outflow was switched on ferocious bubbling masses of water would shoot from the pipes and rush down a concrete slipway into the river. Hence the name given to it by the local children, 'The Rush'. At high tide when the slipway and the pipes were hidden the force of the outflow made the grey waters of the river boil and heave. No one falling into the Rush at high or low tide would stand much chance of survival. Fifty yards upstream from the jetty was the sewerage outfall, a good spot to catch eels and flaties.

On the other side of the Effyl from Riverside, but south of the commercial centre, were the town's main industries; the steelworks, the ship repair dry docks and the yards where sandboats landed their cargoes dredged from the bed of the Bristol Channel. To the north-west on the opposite bank to Riverside was the town centre of Cwmporth with its usual array of shops and some dignified public buildings. Some new office blocks were springing up, but this was a town that largely depended on heavy industry rather than the slipperiness of the financial markets. When David reached the central span of the bridge, he looked south towards the docks, which were in his father's youth overwhelmed with Welsh coal for export. Now, even at this distance the cranes appeared red with rust. Close to the docks, where the iron ore was brought ashore, ran the boundary fence of the steel plant. Its long sheds were covered in a brown haze from the smoke and sulphurous fumes belching from the tall stacks and the blast furnaces. Looping through the site ran railway lines along which rumbled venerable loco's - their high-pitched little hoots and the screech of their brakes sometimes carrying across the river into the heart of Riverside's streets.

Shortly after exiting the ramp of the bridge David Rhys was clocking on at Gate No.1. It was the 18th June 1973, and it was to be the last day for all the blastfurnace men, the loco and charger drivers, the first hands in the melting shop, even for the poor devils always covered in soot and grime and choking on the foul air in the coke plant, and finally for David Rhys as a dolomite.

Pat Rhys came into the scullery and felt the warmth of the fire. Duw! Tom's built it up too much again, she thought. She'd have to bank it down with some small, but she would do so later when her husband had gone to the club to stock up.

-Here you go luv, said Thomas as he handed Pat a mug of tea.

Pat said nothing, and Thomas returned to his seat and was intent on taking refuge in The Daily Mirror. As he opened the paper he stole a quick glance at his wife's face. Yes, he thought, she was still the pretty girl he had married, but she did look awfully tired nowadays. Thomas knew her to be a fun-loving woman at heart and it saddened him to see her now with too many cares, for which, with all the practicality of a woman from the Sirhowy valley, she was determined to take responsibility. Like many such women there was nothing ostentatious about Pat Thomas, who had a neat rather boyish figure, mid-length auburn hair, and warm friendly eyes. Her face was round and still attractive despite the lines that were creeping in. Unusually for most working-class women she looked considerably younger than her actual age of forty six, and she had for a number of years admitted to being no more than thirty nine. Now, however, her gaze was rather stern, and Thomas began to read in earnest. But there was to be no escape.

-And what time do you call it coming in last night then? she asked determinedly.

Thomas Rhys appeared slightly apprehensive, like a roadman unsure of the pit props ahead.

-Hang on now Pat. It wasn't that late, he said defensively.

-And I suppose chairman bloody Hawkins was still there, eh? she said sarcastically.

Taking her husband's silence as confirmation of the late-night drinking presence of Charlie Hawkins, chairman of the Coronation Road Working Men's Club, Pat Thomas proceeded to extract the names of the others.

-Half the bloody committee then, was it? And I suppose they all hung on till the death, swilling it back like there's no tomorrow.

-Well, it was shortly after two when we called it a night, informed Thomas.

-Shortly after two! exploded Pat. Why can't you just shut the bar and bugger 'em? Bugger all the titty men!

This was Pat's way, in private, of referring to the club's committee members. She felt that the term 'titty men' summed them up admirably - small-minded, petty men, who saw women as good for only washing, cooking and screwing. What Pat Rhys did not always recognize was that the committee men - indeed most of the club's members - were frequently people who were treated badly in their own jobs and who, accordingly, handed out similar treatment to a succession of stewards and stewardesses who had worked at the club. For the most part the curmudgeonly attitude towards Thomas and Pat Rhys was the product of a bloody-minded insistence among the majority of the members and especially the committee to ensure value for money for the wages paid to the club's employees. Coupled with this was a dogged determination to insist on the essentially unequal nature of employer-employee relationships, for this was the only occasion when the members enjoyed being in the ascendancy.

-Don't go on so, there's a good girl, urged Thomas. Look, things are not too bad right now. The No. 2 account's on the go nicely, and the committee are too tup to notice anything.

-Aye, but are you sure they're so daft?

-Shush now. Don't worry, said Thomas. They're not going to miss a few bottles of spirits a week now, are they? The dray boys know the score; they won't say anything. The thing is not to get on the wrong side of the committee.

-Or chairman bloody Hawkins either, is it?

-Or him, said Thomas patiently. The club will be in for a rough ride when the works closes, and we'll just have to see it through.

-I know that Tom. But look, if the takings go down someone might get suspicious about the amount of whisky still being sold and...

-Pat! said Thomas abruptly. I'm not doolalley. If the takings drop, I'll order less on my own account. The No. 2 account with the brewery is not fixed by God Almighty, I decide how much the dray boys bring in with the club's order. C'mon now luv. Where'd we be if I packed it in? In the shit, that's where. Christ knows they pay us next to nothing as it is.

-Language Thomas!

Pat disapproved of strong language unless it were "bloody" or "cowing", two epithets frequently applied to the committee men. But in truth she recognized that the extra money brought in by her husband's fiddle was very welcome.

Pat Rhys looked around her small living room. Next to the back door leading into the yard was a small bosh with only a cold-water tap attached precariously to the wall above it. In one corner of the room was an ancient gas cooker; the wallpaper around it was covered in grease and fat marks. The rest of the wallpaper was beginning to peel away around the door jambs. Wallpapers came and went over the years, but the lino' in the scullery never altered. It was always cold to the touch, ragged and chipped at the edges, and boasted a prodigious collection of stains. Occupying lino-space with ill-disguised bulk was a brown three-piece suite, which had once graced the front room before its demotion to the scullery. On the mantelpiece sat a heavy clock, its wood surround now dulled by years of cigarette smoke and fumes from the coal fire. Behind it was stuffed nearly all the important paperwork of the Rhys family; birth certificates, medical cards, insurance book, pools coupon, and the addresses of relatives written on scraps of lined paper. The scullery was a tiny room that screamed decay and pessimism at its inhabitants, but the whole house was slowly peeling away revealing earlier forlorn attempts to make it a bright and decent home. Even with fires lit in both the scullery and the front room - a rare event in most houses in Granall Street and which happened usually only at Christmas or at funerals - the place felt damp. Upstairs, where no fire was ever lit, it was worse, especially in winter when it was not uncommon to see one's breath condense in the cold. To change all this required much more than Thomas Rhys's weekly pay.

-Yes, well, I'm sure you're right Tom, said Pat wistfully. But for Heaven's sake be careful.

-I will. Now don't you be worrying any more, said Thomas who returned to his paper sure that he had weathered the storm.

-And not so late next time those cowing titty men are hanging on, do you hear me? And another thing, I expect you gave 'em a few free pints last night. Well, you can cut that out too.

-Righto luv, conceded Thomas.

Pat's manner had softened considerably now that she had got the late-night drinking and her concern over the No. 2 account off her chest. She got up and stood behind Thomas's chair and ran her fingers gently through the hair on the back of his head.

-Too soft by half you are, Tom Rhys. Too soft by half, she whispered before she went back upstairs to collect the washing.

Thomas smiled, put down his paper, threw some small on the fire to save his wife doing it as he knew she would when he had left for work, and thought about the morning's tasks ahead.

It was nearly midday and David Rhys was returning from the canteen with the first hand's dinner. Each of the oil-powered furnaces in the melting shop, where the actual steel was made, had a crew in order of seniority of first, second, and third hands, and a dolomite. In addition to running errands for the first hand, a dolomite had to make sure that the limestone and sulphur buckets were always full and ready for loading into any of the four furnaces running the length of the shop. There were gaffers, men in white coats, who came onto the shop floor from time to time to oversee the steelmaking, but it was the first and second hands with years of experience who really sorted it all out. Each of these men, with over twenty years in the melting shop, had only to walk up to a furnace and peer through one of the half-opened doors to be able to tell how the mix was coming along. The colour and consistency were what they looked for. Third hands and dolomites usually operated the furnace doors for the charger drivers whose machines loaded bogies full of scrap metal deep into the heart of the fire. In addition, huge quantities of oil and oxygen were pumped into the furnace to slake its thirst so that the length of the melting shop was always filled by the drumming of the oil guns and the roar of the oxi jets.

On an overhead gantry ran a crane with two massive hooked arms to carry the cauldrons of molten iron. When it was time to give a furnace a drink the whole furnace would be tilted backwards slightly, one of the doors would be fully opened, and the crane would position the cauldron and pour in the boiling liquid. At different times during the mix the direction of the oil guns and the oxi jets within the furnace would be switched. Momentarily the noise would decrease, flames and thick acrid smoke would belch from the doors, the pigeons overhead would fly to new positions away from the chaos, and then the furnace would settle down again into its familiar pattern and the drumming and roaring would resume. During these periods the furnace crews would desert the floor of the melting shop and take refuge in their cabins to avoid the thick smoke, which having reached the roof of the shed fell back in the shape of black flakes, called 'tish', and settled on everything. It was part of David's job as a dolomite to clear the cabin of any tish, which may have found its way inside, and to ensure that if the first hand had absent-mindedly left his mug of tea outside it was brought in before the flakes fell.

The dipper man had taken the temperature of 'B' furnace and a thermo sample had been sent off to the lab. In a few minutes the crew would tap her for the last time. Already at the back of the furnace the second hand was chipping away at the seal of gany on the chute. A man in a white coat gave the signal and the furnace was tilted backwards as the final pieces of gany were removed to allow the steel to flow down the chute, like a spurt of lava, into a ladle, which in turn would be hoisted by crane to another bay where the metal was teemed into separate moulds accompanied each time by small explosions of sparks and pops. After a few minutes, while the whole crew of 'B' furnace stood looking on, the tapping was complete and the mechanism was set back on an even keel, all the guns were turned off, and her insides were allowed slowly to cool like the other three furnaces that had been pensioned off earlier. In a couple of weeks, the scrap men would be about their business crawling all over her and taking her to pieces.

David wiped away some of the thin film of white limestone dust from his brow. She had been a good furnace, he thought. Away from the cold and the wind in winter, tucked as she was towards the centre of the floor and thus some distance from the open ends of the melting shop where the loco's chugged in an out with their loads of scrap and wagons of minerals. Even now with the dust and grime in his hair he still felt that it had been a good job. He worked with a good bunch whom he respected, especially the first hands who seemed unaffected by the fierceness of the furnace's naked heat and who were able to saunter right upto an open door as if inspecting their own coal fire at home. Getting too close to the furnace, such as when you had to throw aluminium in by shovel, was just about the only part of the job he hadn't liked. That and perhaps the 'stinkers' - the foul pinching smell of sulphur, a substance that was used extensively in making certain kinds of steel. But the rest had all been fine. Even the tatty cabins with their hard bench seats were like a home from home where you could get a cuppa, have a game of cards during quiet times, and always find a mate to chat with.

The pigeons high in the blackened roof of the melting shop were perched on the beams uncertainly, thrown into doubt by the unusual stillness. David looked at the worn controls of the furnace doors, the charger vehicles and the gantry crane parked forlornly at one end of the melting shop, and he watched the small band of steelmen slowly walk away towards the shower block. He joined them inside where some quiet cheerios were said, and soon after he emerged into the daylight. Reaching the bridge, he looked back at the Sceptre Works. There was no more falling tish, no more drumming and roaring of furnaces, no more dolomites covered in dust heading for the canteen to pick up fried egg sandwiches. Even the smell of sulphur in the air was not as strong as usual and tomorrow that too would have disappeared. Beneath him the Effyl flowed on, its clouded waters slipping past the muddy flanks.

CHAPTER TWO

The prim letter in its brown envelope, which had dropped solemnly through the letter-box, had given David an early morning signing-on time. The first few weeks on the dole had not been so bad. Of course, you couldn't really live on what they gave you, but the redundancy money eased the pressure. It was a bright July day and already the sunlight was casting deep shadows along Granall Street. The schools had just broken up and there were knots of children along the street planning their various campaigns, for the summer holidays were not to be frittered away. There were fishing expeditions to be arranged along the Effyl; great bicycle treks to be attempted all the way to the coast itself; and forays into far-flung parks in other parts of the town to be ventured. For the younger children hop-scotch lines were to be drawn; the venue for the marble matches awaited decision; and skipping routines and songs had to be mutually agreed.

As David stepped out of the house, he saw a group of four boys quickly agree the permitted boundaries in which a game of marbles was about to be played, and then witnessed some heated disagreement whether the match - so early in the day before fingers became properly nimble - should be for 'keepsies' or merely 'lendsies'. A compromise was soon arranged in which it was hands-on-hearts avowed that ordinary marbles lost in the contest might be kept permanently by the victor, but special alleys suffering such a fate had to be returned to the rightful owner at the game's conclusion. The contest started in the gutter outside David's house and soon one of the combatants was faced with a tricky shot. An opponent's marble could easily be struck and captured, but it was the weight of the shot that was the problem. The target marble was perilously close to the boundary - a drain cover. Too hard a shot might mean losing one's prize down the drain, or worse, losing both marbles. In the event, the shot was skilfully executed and the shiny marble with the bright red centre was gleefully pocketed.

In summer the stagnant water and debris in the drains gave off a festering smell, which prompted many of the mothers in the street to circulate fantastic stories to try to keep their children away from any health danger. The latest cautionary tale was that you could catch some awful disease by breathing the foul air emitted from the drains. However, if the children ever believed such a story, they certainly showed more concern about keeping their marbles out of the drains than keeping in the sickness-inducing vapours. David would have stayed a while longer to watch the contest unfold, but the scruffy boy who had lost the red marble gave him an annoyed glance in a successful attempt to move David on.

The dole office was at the top end of Coronation Road but it could be reached by a dirt track that skirted the river, and it was this latter route David decided to follow. Leaving Granall Street and turning left into Dankley Alley, David soon found himself strolling along the river's edge. There were no children, as yet, fishing along the banks of the Effyl, for they were all still digging in their own, or anyone else's, back gardens in search of worms. The recent warm dry weather was making it hard work to find sufficient bait for a day's sport. Three men, who had bought some ragworm from a tackle shop, were just setting up their gear on the landing stage. In the shade cast by the central span of the suspension bridge David met Old Man Morgan. In Riverside everyone called him Old Man Morgan, not to his face, mind; in person you called him Mr. Morgan. No one knew his first name so Mr. Morgan it was face-to-face, and Old Man Morgan at all other times.

-Morning me lad, he offered in a gruff but not unkindly manner.

-Morning Mr. Morgan, said David respectfully. Off anywhere special?

-No lad, he sighed. I just wanted to get out of the house while me legs feel able to carry me. I gets bored being cooped up for too long.

-I thought you spent a lot o' time with your pigeons, said David sympathetically.

-Used to. But I can't get about now to feed 'em and muck 'em out, so they had to go.

The thought of that day, when he had wrung the necks of his precious birds, made his eyes well with tears, which only with a supreme effort did Old Man Morgan prevent from flowing down his face - a face that was sad and lined beyond measure. You could see then that he was old, very old, as if he'd always been that way and had been practising the bent frame and the unsteady gait all his life. Old Man Morgan was seventy-nine and a widower for the past six years. It was confidently said by many in Granall Street that he had two sons who lived up Doncaster way, but no one ever came to the house. While his mind was still quick, physically he was coming apart at the seams, just like much of his old clothing. His walking stick was the only solid thing about him.

-I'd better be getting back, said Old Man Morgan looking at a pocket watch he extracted with some difficulty from a worn waistcoat.

On the end of the albert was a cup-winners medal inscribed 'Cwmporth AFC, County Cup, 1913', but no one ever noticed it nor asked about it.

-Will you be okay? said David.

-The legs haven't gone yet. I'll be fine.

Slowly the old man turned and headed towards Granall Street, his walking stick searching out a sure footing on the uneven gravel.

David walked on a few paces until he was between the landing stage and the sewerage outfall. The high tide was about to turn and the men on the jetty would have some good fishing as the debris from the sewer flowed towards them like a kind of ground bait. Rod tips glinted against the dappled water and across the river the sun caught the silent towers of the blast furnaces in the Sceptre Works. One of the men cast out and David watched the high arching trajectory of the paternoster and he could clearly see the splash of the weighted line in midstream. Swiftly the current caught the line and pulled it taut, and the man sat back patiently to wait, occasionally turning and chatting to his two friends.

The Effyl was beginning to flow more purposefully towards the sea for it was a large tide that day. At such times the channel was both broad and deep, and the intricate eddies and swirls all spoke of the river's power. Large swathes of soft dark mud along the river's steep flanks were being uncovered as the tide raced away. The river was not just a channel for the water, heavy with silt and industrial pollution, it was also a local dumping ground - a gully whose glutinous mud willingly accommodated the iron stoves, car tyres, and clapped-out prams that were abandoned there. When the river was in full-throat rushing to and from a mighty high tide, it was capable of scouring its banks of much of this debris, so that the jigsaw of cast-offs and household junk was ever changing. Often, a dead sheep, claimed much higher up along the river's course, would be washed along bobbing up and down with its straggly hair looking like a discarded mop. Sometimes, it would be beached just below the topmost grass embankment, where the tides reached only occasionally, and the smell of putrefaction would linger for weeks.

A small number of circles of blackened earth along the embankment told where bonfires had been lit, made up with drift wood left by the tide. Many of the children and teenagers from Granall and Ribley streets, whose creations these bonfires were, attended the summer evenings' festivities, but the older boys would do their best to drive the youngsters away so that they could devote all their attention to the local talent. They tried to impress the girls by stripping off to their underpants and diving from the landing stage into the turbid waters, or else walking around the fire in a handstand, or - best of all as far as the girls were concerned - jumping through the flames so that their lean bodies glistened in the flickering light.

In the distance four figures, three youths and a girl, emerged from the Brownhills and walked along the river embankment towards the landing stage. As they approached, David could make them out as three lads from Ribley Street, who answered to the nicknames of Plod, Stomper, and Cavie. They were all a few years older than the fourteen-year-old girl, Elaine Roberts, who was hanging around with them. Plod, the eldest of the bunch and the self-appointed leader, was eighteen and, like David, was on his way to sign on. As they came to a point level with the end of Dankley Alley they climbed up from the grass embankment onto the dirt track and continued on their way in David's direction. They were joined by the ragged figure of Peety Malone who walked a few paces behind the others, constantly tucking in his ill-fitting pullover, inspecting his trouser buttons - one of which was undone allowing a piece of his shirt to poke through - and softly speaking to himself. The others were completely at ease with this strange behaviour.

-What're you doing later? Cavie asked Elaine who, on a whim, decided to ignore this squat, mousy-haired lad who had furtively detached himself from the others.

-She ain't going nowhere with you, laughed Stomper.

Where Cavie was thick in body and mind, and Plod had a powerful muscular appearance and a cynicism to match, Stomper was altogether slimmer and more intelligent. He looked down on Cavie as the butt of his jokes, but he lacked the physical prowess and sheer head-banging courage of Plod, which in Riverside was what made Plod the group's leader and not any of the others.

-She'd have to be blind wanting to go anywhere with you, you ugly sod, continued Stomper in a manner that was not altogether friendly ragging as far as Cavie was concerned.

Cavie felt that he ought to make some response.

-Piss off, you bag of piss, came his entirely unimaginative rejoinder.

-Stow it you two! ordered Plod who was feeling in the pocket of his greasy leather jacket.

His pale face always grew serious when he asserted his authority and sometimes the veins would stand out on his neck so that the tattoo on his left side, which simply said 'war', seemed to throb with expectation. Despite his tall and powerful frame, and his observant blue eyes, there was a nervousness and a restlessness about Plod that made many people feel uneasy in his company.

-Shit! exclaimed Plod when he realized he was out of cigarettes.

He knew that neither of his mates had any. Elaine might have, but he felt he would lose face if he asked her for a fag. He did not entirely approve of this skinny little kid tagging along like this, but there was something about her - a sensuality, a possibility of compliance - that stopped him from sending her away. Plod turned to Peety Malone.

-Peety! Here take this money and run down to Joneses. Bring me back five No.6. We'll be heading for the sandyards, so you can catch us up before we get to the dole office.

It was as if Plod had addressed his demand to a child, but Peety was thirty-five years old. Even so he did exactly as he was told and set off to get the cigarettes. Mrs. Jones would split a packet and put five fags in a paper bag. She knew Peety well for he was always in and out of her shop as he ran errands for people in Granall Street and the surrounding area. You could trust Peety despite the fact that he had a limited understanding of the world. He always brought back the correct change and it was only the very complicated errands he occasionally got wrong. Despite the fact that he was forever a thirty-five-year-old child, or because of it, people in Riverside liked Peety Malone; he was a recognized part of the place. He didn't look normal, mind you. In fact, he looked doltish and was always unshaven. His shabby appearance was made worse by his mam's insistence on dressing him in second-hand clothes that were always too big for him so that he seemed to be fighting a daily battle to bring his attire under some semblance of control. His hair was black and spiky and was cut with all the charm associated with the pudding bowl approach to hairstyling. He also had his funny ways, and to an outsider his habit of suddenly shaking his head violently, like some stallion that had just won a race, could be very off-putting. But since Peety ventured hardly at all outside Riverside, he rarely embarrassed anyone.

Yes, Peety Malone was well-liked within Riverside; indeed, he had his allotted place within the social ebb and flow of the terraced streets.

Everyone knew he was not all there. All the children, in fact, could tell you why he was so tup: it was because an earwig had crawled into his ear when he was a baby and, unnoticed, it had burrowed through to his brain. But of all the potential playmates in the street no one was more reliable than Peety. Any child had only to issue the challenge 'pull Peety' for Peety to throw himself into a gunslinger's crouch, draw his imaginary six-shooter out of the holster, aim at the challenger, shout 'blam', and then blow the smoke away before returning his index finger to the holster after having seen off yet another rival. And you could do this any number of times; you could call 'pull Peety' in the middle of a howling gale, or as the vaunted gunman was attending to an errand, or as he was lighting a cigarette, and he would always draw on you and go through the same actions. Trustworthy and reliable that was Peety Malone.

The little group watched Peety until he turned out of view and then they resumed their journey - Cavie trying to get close to Elaine once again (even daring to touch her long fair hair); Stomper awaiting the chance to impress the girl with another put-down; and Plod growing more resentful, of what he was not sure, but feeling that something would have to give soon. The three youths, but not Elaine, acknowledged David with a few nods and cursory hellos. They walked past and soon they were no more than specks on the dirt track in the hazy distance.

Thomas Rhys had just carried up to the bar the last case of Mackies from the bottle shed in the yard. There had been a good crowd in last night and so there was a lot of stocking up to do. It was quite a journey back and forth between the shed and the bar, and Thomas sat down to have a smoke before putting the bottles on the shelf. His wife worked mostly evenings and, unless David gave him a hand with the stocking up or the pump cleaning, all the morning's work before the club opened, he had to do on his own. Carrying up the cases of bottles wasn't too bad. Although this had to be done every day, it was steady effort and Thomas could always take a break. Cleaning the pumps and the pipes, which he did each week, was a regular chore that could not be missed because the beer would soon acquire a sour taste. Quite rightly people would complain and say the beer tasted "off". But cleaning the pipes wasn't too bad either. It wasn't physically demanding, just time-consuming because of the amount of fresh water that had to be pulled through the hand-pumps to flush out the 'Presto' cleaning solution. It was the cellar work that was the real killer.

Most of the beer still consumed in the club was bitter or mild - proper beer, not your gassed-up golden sparkling stuff. If it was not to turn cloudy or bitty in the glass it required looking after and proper preparation before it could be drawn. Good cellarage was of the essence. But the cellar at the Coronation Road Working Men's Club and Institute was little more than a long narrow trench cut below the bar and ending underneath the pavement of Coronation Road where the dray delivered the barrels. On one of his busman's holidays to have a drink at a neighbouring club Thomas had been shown around his fellow steward's cellar. It was like a large vault with whitewashed walls, individual blocks and trestles for the barrels, and a proper air circulation system; it was so big it even had a skittle alley down one side. In contrast, the cellar in which Thomas worked his art was damp, dingy, and cramped. Although the brick-walled cavity was sixty feet long, it was only ten feet wide. Down the middle ran a small passageway with barely enough room for a man to turn around, and on either side of this was a three-and-a-half-foot high concrete shelf on which sat the beer barrels. At six foot one and a half inches, Thomas Rhys was several inches taller than the height of the cellar, so that with the exception of the areas by the delivery ramp and the stairs into the cellar from the bar he was constantly forced to walk in a stoop or with his head cocked over unnaturally to one side. He had worked in cramped and awkward places before as a miner, but the physical layout of the club's cellar made many demands on his strength and ingenuity. The final indignity of this ungodly hole was that the drain in the floor, which let out the water used to sluice down the shelves and the passageway, was sometimes sufficiently vindictive to let river water in. This happened every other year or so when a high tide coincided with heavy rain and there was a backflow of foul water through congested sewers into below ground areas like the cellar. On such occasions, Thomas was powerless to prevent his barrels of beer setting sail on this overwhelming tide of filth that invaded the confines of the cellar.

It was not all bad, however. Getting the empty barrels out of the cellar was no problem; the dray boys simply hauled the empties up the wooden ramp with ropes wrapped around the barrels' flanks. But Thomas had to be careful about the full ones coming in. The dray boys were strong men, but sometimes ropes slipped and heavy barrels had been known to come thundering down the ramp. All Thomas could do then was duck under them in the passageway and watch helplessly as they smashed into other barrels on the shelves. Thomas had to be careful too in other ways. While the plastic pipes could be connected to barrels anywhere in the cellar, it was better to have barrels in use on a short length of piping as close to the bar pumps as possible. This meant preparing barrels for immediate use at the top end of the cellar by the stairs and flap door into the bar. Thomas always told the dray boys to send down first five wooden barrels of best bitter and then two casks of mild so that he could position these along the two shelves at the top end of the cellar. Various metal kegs of lager and gassed-up beer would come next, followed finally by extra barrels of bitter and of mild. However, if there were heavier demand than normal for bitter or mild so that the front-loaded barrels had been emptied, Thomas would have to manhaul others from the bottom of the cellar to the top. The barrels in the way had to be lifted across to spaces on the other shelf, and with full barrels of beer this was backbreaking work.

There was no dray delivery today, thought Thomas thankfully. A sudden bout of coughing caused him to stub out his cigarette. When he had regained his composure and he no longer felt so breathless he put the bottles of Mackeson in their usual place. He wondered whether to bring up another soda bottle and then remembered that Tony Newbold, the club treasurer, would not be in for he was off to the races. He was one of only a few customers who called for soda in his whisky. It was getting on for 9.15 am; just time, thought Thomas, to do the pipes before open tap at 11 o'clock. Returning from the cellar where he had turned off the barrel taps, Thomas removed all the thrifty trays from each of the three sets of hand pumps and pulled off the remaining beer in the pipes. The bitter and the mild were drawn off into separate stainless-steel pails to be filtered back into their respective barrels later. Then he fetched the 'Presto' from the cwtsh under the stairs and mixed the powder with hot water in three large white enamelled buckets. One by one Thomas carried the buckets down the steep stairs to the cellar where their pungent caustic smell masked the normal odour of hops. He disconnected the pipes from the barrels and placed them two at a time into each of the three buckets. Then Thomas returned to the bar where he pulled the cleaning solution through the pumps until the whole length of each of the pipes was full. It had to be left in the pipes for twenty minutes during which time Thomas cleared away the old spiles, corks, and filter papers from the cellar. When the pipes had had a good soak the ends of all six were placed in a large sink at the side of the cellar into which a tap supplied a good flow of clean cold water. From then on Thomas spent over an hour pulling gallon after gallon of fresh water through the pipes and pumps to ensure the removal of the last traces of 'Presto'. Each bucket he filled had to be emptied at the sink in the bar and it was ten minutes to eleven o'clock before the whole laborious process was finished, and Thomas just had enough time to reconnect the pipes, replace the thrifty trays, and pull through the beer ready for the morning's first customers.

Mary O'Flaherty was one of those women everyone called 'the salt of the earth'. She looked as if she had actually tilled the soil for her face was red and blotchy like that of a peasant's. She had a girth too that indicated a more than passing acquaintance with potatoes and strong drink. Or perhaps it was her salty language that had earned her this description. Certainly, her husband, Dec, was often seen to be on the receiving end of her sharp tongue. More likely it was her unbowed optimism, her willingness to muck in, and her sod-em-all attitude when things went badly that people recognized. She was always the first round nearly every door taking a collection on behalf of the bereaved whenever someone in Granall Street had died. If there were a street party to organize, she would be in the thick of it, her booming voice directing one and all.

-Usual Tom, said Mary in the confident way that club regulars have when ordering their tipple.

The tipple in question, of a morning, was port and lemon, but Mary gravitated towards gin and lime of an evening.

-And some change, said Mary who waited quietly sipping her drink while Thomas counted out the ten pence pieces.

-Did it drop last night? asked Mary indicating with a backward jerk of her head the one-armed bandit at the rear of the club. Betty was giving it a good bash, she continued, and twice she got 'tic tac', but no sodding 'toe'.

-No. No one got the jackpot last night, said Thomas somewhat wearily as he turned away to count the number of bags of coin in the safe.

Picking up her glass, Mary headed straight to the bandit. She would play it for the next hour or so until she had to pop back home through the alleyway at the back of the club to get her kids something to eat. She might be joined by Betty Sawyer and Jean Evans who often dropped in for a while during the mornings, but if truth be told she preferred to play on her own. It was better that way; she could get a good rhythm going, feeding the coins into the insatiable slot, hearing them drop with their distinctive clink and whirr, and holding the handle and pulling it down with the same firm and easy stroke. Then as the handle sprang back the three circles of fortune would spin, coming to a breathtaking halt in quick succession - clunk, a cherry - clunk, another cherry (that's fifty pence whatever happens) - clunk, an orange (Shit! Missed it. But so close). She was trying to sense the machine's mood that day. Was it going to start paying out piffling little amounts, or were there real chances for a big drop; maybe the jackpot worth at least twenty quid? Mary worked the machine to some inner expectation, now and then sipping her drink, sometimes cursing her luck, and more and more depleting her slender winnings from the pay-out slot. There would be no jackpot today but Mary played on regardless.

From the little serving hatch at the back of the bar Thomas Rhys briefly watched the Jennings machine swallow some more of Mary's money. Then he returned to his accounts, being interrupted occasionally to serve the handful of members who were spread around the club reading the papers or staring at the smoke-yellowed walls. The downstairs room of the club was long and split into two uneven parts by the bar. It was an old-fashioned bar with heavy wooden shutters containing panes of frosted glass, which had to be pulled down and individually locked when Thomas and Pat closed up at night. Being built right upto a partition wall, the bar had only three sides where customers could be served, and one of these contained no more than a hatch, which faced the smaller end of the club and the toilets. Down the other side of the bar ran the skittle alley, but unless there was a match being played the alley was normally covered by tables and chairs. The rest of the front part of the club was used for bingo sessions and once a month or so some of the furniture was pushed back to allow for dancing. The stairs, located along the partition wall behind the bar, led to a so-called concert room, which was unused and virtually derelict, and to the committee room.

All the furniture downstairs was made of dark brown wood, which was battered and bore the marks of many cigarette burns. The walls were undecorated save for an old portrait of the Queen, but they were made more interesting by the tidemarks they contained. The club's cleaning lady was old and short, and where she had tried to wipe away some of the years of accumulated beer and smoke stains, she had only succeeded in leaving a series of crescents, above which the grime clung with undisturbed serenity and below which the original colour of the walls could very faintly be discerned. It added to the overall down-at-heel appearance, but few of the members seemed to mind. They came here to drink after all; and the beer was cheap. They came here to talk to friends; and the talk too was often cheap for on most nights you could usually find a few where the beer was doing the talking for them.

There were no smoke extractors except the front and back doors but there was, however, central heating. This was fuelled by an old coke-fired stove that lived next to the stairs. During the winter evenings it was supposed to be the responsibility of the committee members to keep the stove going. A rota was drawn up but seldom honoured, and eventually chairman Hawkins felt that it was undignified for him to have to carry through buckets of coke from the bunker in the yard, and the job was dumped on the steward. In turn, on those nights when the club was very busy and the steward could not easily leave the bar to collect the coke, Thomas would ask the old boy on the door - who signed in the guests - if he'd throw on some buckets, and Thomas would give him a few free pints in return. If the club had one rule, to which it adhered strongly, it was that nothing should be allowed to get in the way of the drinking and socializing. It was that sort of place, and to ensure that nothing did get in the way a committee and chairman were elected to run the club.

What a wondrous institution is the committee of a working men's club. At the Coronation Road club everyone had a vote in the election of the committee members; everyone that is except women who were only associate members and they could neither vote nor stand for the committee. Among the all-male committee were a few decent blokes, but mostly they were men who liked the sound of their own voices, had opinions on everything under the sun, and thought they knew better than anyone how to run a club. In fact, as Thomas was very fond of telling his son, most of them couldn't organize a piss-up in a brewery.

The club secretary was Alf Smith, a small spectacled man in his late forties who took his orders from Charlie Hawkins, the chairman. Tony Newbold, the treasurer, enjoyed some measure of independence from the chairman because Charlie as well as being practically illiterate was also innumerate. Despite these handicaps the chairman owed his position of authority to his willingness to take on board those jobs he liked doing, particularly calling the bingo numbers and getting concert nights going with his loud renditions of Tom Jones and Frank Sinatra ballads, and generally to his eagerness to call the shots over small issues such as replacing the dart board, ordering more French chalk for the dance floor, and fixing the leaking tap in the ladies toilet. He felt that sending the bills for some of these things to Tony Newbold gave him the upper hand over someone he both envied and distrusted. Envied because Tony was taller and certainly more handsome. Distrusted because of the younger man's facility with money and his altogether flash appearance. The fifty-year-old chairman was anything other than flash; he was simply dowdy and fat. In fact, he was a great slob of a man, so much so that it was one of the mysteries of the neighbourhood why Jean Evans, his common law wife, ever put up with him. Jean worked as a part-time usherette at the Roxy cinema but it was not only lack of cash that kept her with Charlie Hawkins, it was also the bullying and occasional backhander across the face that made her too frightened to leave. Jean dreaded Charlie receiving any humiliation at the club, however slight, whether actual or perceived, for she knew he would take it out on her later. As far as Charlie himself was concerned, he felt that Jean was always nagging him at home, while at work however sullenly he had to do as he was told. It was only inside the crumbling walls of the Coronation Road Working Men's Club and Institute - *his* club - that Charlie Hawkins believed he walked tall.

Around one o'clock Charlie made his entrance into the club. He hung his work coat by the front door and surveyed who was in. Betty Sawyer and Jean were playing the bandit and at the front of the bar were a couple of committee men, Frank Harris and Bert Price. Charlie nodded to them as he reached the counter where Thomas served him with a pint of bitter. Charlie held the glass up to the light and ostentatiously inspected the brew, then he slapped the right money on the counter and joined Frank and Bert. Both men had worked in the rolling mill at the Sceptre Works and permanent unemployment now stretched before them because there were no jobs any longer in Cwmporth for men in their fifties with such specialized skills.

-Just had a bloody grueller, said Charlie after he had downed half his pint in one go.

Frank and Bert stared into their beers too embarrassed to say anything. Charlie Hawkins was a sweeper-up and cleaner at a wagon repair factory. How could anyone have a hard day pushing a brush around they asked themselves silently.

-Eight o'clock sharp tonight then lads, said Charlie in reference to the weekly committee meeting.

-Aye. We'll be there, volunteered Bert for the two of them.

-So, tell us mun, is there anything interesting coming up tonight? asked Frank.

Charlie was sitting with his back to the bar. He glanced over his shoulder quickly and saw that Thomas was serving a customer; he drew his chair nearer to the table and hunched his heavy frame closer to the others.

-Well, there's the little matter of the steward and stewardess's time off.

Frank felt uncomfortable but he replied in a half whisper.

-They have Wednesday night off together. What's wrong with that?

-Better if one of them was yere all the time 'case the beer goes off. The barmaid doesn't always know how to change the barrel over, said Charlie.

-Tom normally has a fresh barrel all lined up before they go out, argued Bert.

Charlie wasn't going to stand any nonsense, especially where the cardinal rule of the club was involved.

-You say. But I've 'ad to wait a long while before now while some stupid cow of a girl tries to change 'em over. Look, it's on the card for tonight. We'll sort it then.

With no more ado Charlie drank up and on his way out the back door uttered a few harsh comments to Jean about his dinner being ready when he got home. Jean rather apologetically took her share of the winnings from the pile by the side of Betty's handbag and hurried off to Ribley Street in the hope that she would get there before him.

In the evening, under the prompting of Charlie Hawkins but not without some opposition, the committee decided that the weekly night off together enjoyed by Pat and Thomas Rhys would cease. Henceforth, they were to take separate evenings off. The decision did not surprise Thomas for between Charlie and him there had always been a mutual distaste. The chairman hated the steward because Thomas would not bend the knee; he would not kow-tow. Thomas Rhys had been something proud and decent in his working life. For the slugs of this world, like Charlie Hawkins, Thomas Rhys could only feel contempt and the overwhelming determination not to sink to his level. But Pat Rhys was appalled at the decision. It seemed to her to be yet another nail in the struggle to lead some semblance of a normal family life. The chairman of the titty men had dealt another cruel blow to the hopes of Pat Rhys.

CHAPTER THREE

A long restless queue of children snaked its way towards the small stage under the portrait of the Queen. There each child was given an apple, an orange, a bag of crisps (plain only), a cheap novelty toy, and a few bob to spend at the fair for today was the club outing to Barry Island. Although it was early morning drinks were being served at the bar and the club was full of families. Children ran to their parents to show off their gifts; mothers pulled out paper hankies from carrier bags, which also contained home-made sandwiches, bottles of pop, and plastic macs, and wiped away the snot from their children's faces; men shouted hearty greetings to other men and rolled their eyes in mock horror at the endless machinations of their wives and kids; women quietly scolded husbands and reminded them to go easy on the beer.

Suddenly Charlie Hawkins's voice could be heard above the din calling for strong men to carry the cases of beer to the coaches parked along much of the length of Granall Street. Having gathered his band, the chairman led them to the bottle shed where Thomas pointed out the cases to be loaded. Like a line of sherpas, they filed through the yard and the alleyway into the street where Charlie, who had carried nothing at all, took command once more and sent men and their cases to the twelve coaches and did his best to ensure that each one was allocated a fair share of the drink. It was supposed to last there and back, but most of the coaches ran out of booze comfortably before they arrived at the resort. The drivers stood around in a lethargic knot smoking and letting the sherpas and their leader get on with it. The coaches they drove were long past the stage when it was necessary to look after the upholstery. Anyway, it wasn't the men having a drink that bothered them; it was the kids, some of whom thought it was actually funny to be sick down the back of a driver's neck.

The usual pattern was unfolding for the club's annual August trip to the seaside. Members and their families started to turn up at the club for the children's presents around nine o'clock. By half past the place was mayhem and not just in the club for the whole street would be out - adults on their doorsteps urging everyone to have a good time as they boarded the buses, and children running in between the parked coaches and jumping up at the windows to make faces at those inside. These children who danced merrily around the vehicles were the ones whose parents did not belong to the club and so could not go on the trip. There was, however, one exception. Betty Sawyer always took Peety Malone. One year a committee man had challenged her about this - Mrs Malone was a teetotaller to whom the very idea of even setting foot inside the Coronation Road Working Men's Club was most upsetting. Betty's sharp response had been to tell the committee man that she spent a damn sight more in the club than the cost of an apple, orange, and mouldy packet of crisps. Although Peety's mother would not countenance the idea of him going inside the club, she did allow Peety to join the outing and Betty insisted on getting his presents herself. Peety was already on-board coach No.3 where, between eating his crisps and failing to recognize the purpose of his novelty toy, he had shot down several children who had issued the usual challenge.

The club was beginning to empty as people were called to the coaches. Soon Thomas and Pat had only a few customers to serve, some blokes who were never going to the Island in the first place, but who had called in to take advantage of the early open tap. Around them was the debris of crisp papers and orange peel.

-I'll sweep it up mam, came the unexpected offer from David.

The commotion below his bedroom window had woken David who had dressed and gone outside just in time to see the first bus leaving the street, its windows full of laughing faces and waving arms.

-Sure? asked Pat.

She was feeling both sad and angry that the simple pleasures afforded to the club members - a happy-go-lucky family outing - had once again been denied her own family, as had so often been the case in the past. For a moment she experienced an intense loathing of the club and its grubby walls and loud-mouthed members. She resented bitterly that she and her husband were tied to the place; she felt she had to get away if only for a short while. But in the next moment her sense of practical duty reasserted itself and she knew there was nowhere to go.

-Alright then, I've got some shopping to do anyway, said Pat at last in response to David's offer.

His father handed him the broom and David swept the floor clean, careful to sweep around the few members still in the room who were now enjoying the silence. Throwing the rubbish into the unlit stove and returning the broom to the cwtsh, David joined his father behind the bar.

The flap door into the cellar was open and Thomas sat next to it smoking his cigarette and staring at the barrels below. Thomas Rhys had large hands with long fingers, several of which were misshapen. It had been a childhood habit of David's that no matter how many times his father explained to him how his fingers became so bent, he would ask him again to tell him. In fact, it was David's way of getting his father to talk about his life underground - not his job or his work, mark you, but his life. Before the war and before nationalization of the pits Thomas had been a coal hewer, one of the underground elite. He had worked in dangerous and confined places; he had held his own dying brother in his arms at the bottom of the mine shaft after a piece of metal falling the length of the shaft had hit him and taken half his head away. He had heard an overseer tell another miner following a brake failure on one of the heavily laden trams of coal, which had run downhill out of control and crushed a pit pony, that it would have been better had it been him killed and not the horse. Men were easier to replace. Thomas had broken several fingers in minor accidents while at the coal face, and he had worked on because he needed the pay; and if you did not work, they did not pay you. The pit where he'd toiled all those years ago was called in Welsh, Ty-Trist - 'sad house'.

-you need any of the barrels shifting? asked David.

-No thanks.

Thomas's warm brown eyes looked fondly on his son. He takes after his mother, he thought. The smattering of customers supped their beer contentedly and presented Thomas with an opportunity to speak to David about a matter he had wanted to bring up for a while.

-You're a good lad you know. I'd always wanted something better for you than the mines or this.

Thomas Rhys raised his head slowly to survey the club. There was a distinct look of regret on his face as David watched his father closely. He's getting old; and in a brutal fashion it occurred to David that his father seemed very tired.

-I'd hoped you'd stay on at school, continued Thomas. You were so good at a number of subjects mun; and now there don't seem a lot of promise round yere what with the steelworks closing.

-We've been all over that dad. It's past now. Look, I'm young; something will turn up.

-So was I once, and look what turned up for me. The second world war!

They smiled at one another affectionately. They both knew that Thomas could get really worked up talking about the war and the Welsh Guards, so much so that Pat was fond of saying that though she had never seen a tank, she was sure she could get in one now and drive the bloody thing away. For all the fact that Pat did sometimes find his stories about wartime events and friends a little tedious, she was proud of her husband; they didn't let just anybody join the Guards.

-You sure about the barrels are you then dad? said David in a manner that indicated that he was about to leave.

-Yes. You get on you. There's nothing much yere to do. I'll see you later on, is it?

The tiredness, which never seemed to go away nowadays, caused Thomas's body to ache with the effort simply of sitting upright. It was not the right moment to talk about his son's future; it would have to wait for a while longer.

David nodded to his father and left. He thought about returning to the house, but the certainty of moping around with nothing to do depressed him, and he decided instead to go for a walk.

Smelly Park, as everyone in Riverside called it, was not much of a place - a couple of football and rugby pitches, some swings, a slide, and a roundabout - but it was the only green open space in the district. Down one side of the park was a glue factory where you could see the dead animals being driven in through the entrance. Sandwiched between the factory and the river were the Brownhills, which had been the site of an old chemical works and which was now a general dumping ground. Children often scrambled on their bikes over the landscape of copper-coloured mounds and gravel hillocks or sought out newts and taddies in the small ponds still scattered around the area.

Two stray mongrels were sniffing about the posts of the slide when David arrived at Smelly Park. He saw one of a group children who had been playing Cowboys and Indians shoo them away. The dogs quickly retreated a few paces and then turned to weigh up their adversary. One of them barked, which prompted the child to pick up a stone and throw it at the offending creature. The animals ran off and the children were left in peace again to enjoy their game. On the park's only seat, located in glorious isolation between the rugby and football pitches, David could see Old Man Morgan. He sat stiffly with his cane at his side and was watching the traffic in the distance moving along Coronation Road.

David continued his walk towards the Brownhills with the intention of reaching the river and returning home via the embankment and Dankley Alley. The Brownhills were deserted and derelict. A faint smell, different from that of the glue factory and of the sulphurous odour of the steelworks, hung in the still air. It was like the smell of soot being brushed from a chimney. On some of the hillocks and in a

few of the hollows a coarse yellowy grass was pushing through the gravel. David walked half-way up one of the mounds and leant against a rusting iron mangle, which having been dumped there years ago now seemed to have taken root. Despite the ugliness of the surroundings, it was peaceful, but David could not help feeling anxious. It was an anxiety that had been with him for some while, which at first he put down to the works closing and to the uncertainty about future employment. But it was more than that, and lately it had become almost palpable like a knot in his stomach. It was tightening and then relaxing, tightening and relaxing, moving to forces and events that he was now trying to make clear in his mind.

He could not pinpoint any dramatic change that had occurred. It was more subtle than that, like being in a room and hearing a low continuous noise, knowing it was there, but not being able to trace it exactly so that after a while you begin to doubt your own senses, and it is only if the noise stops that you can be sure again that you really did hear it. David looked about him; he was still alone in the midst of the dereliction. Suddenly, as if a troublesome noise within his own mind had ceased, he began to recognize what was bothering him. Being thrown out of work meant (among other things) that David was spending more time at home and in the club talking to his parents than at any other time since he was a child. For the first time as an adult he was witnessing the kind of lives his parents actually lived. David knew his father wanted him to get on and to do well, and he sensed that his mother's hopes for them all as a family were slowly dissolving. For years, David recalled, she had been pestering the club to build a proper kitchen onto the back of the scullery. But asking committee men to spend their money on the club's employees was almost in the realms of the absurd. So, she was still slaving away over a tiny cooker stuck in the corner. In addition, she wanted one of those fancy gas-fires instead of the old grate and fireplace, but the committee would not give its permission for the old fittings to be torn out. When he was a child, he thought his parents simply worked for a living like everyone else's, but now he could see that for them the club and its punishing routine had become a war of attrition. The palpitating knot in his stomach was the awful recognition that for the first time they were being worn down too far and that his father was no longer the robust and strong man he had always known.

David remembered that when he was a child, he was often woken by the noise of the last club members going home through the alleyway, part of which was under his bedroom. In Granall Street their boozy goodnights would continue and often they would carry on talking under the lamppost outside David's house. Occasionally he would hear them making nasty remarks about his father. Some of these men bitching about something or other his father was supposed to have done were the same men who a few days later would be tapping him for the loan of a few pounds till pay-day. And because he was good-hearted and generous, he'd give it to them, only to be told off later by his wife for being too soft. Every now and then there'd be a fight between two or more members and if it happened in the narrow confines of the alleyway itself the sound of the blows and the foul language would echo around David's room. Then his father would have to come down from the club and sort it out, which meant sorting out the fighters themselves. You could be bloody sure none of the titty men would be around for it was an unwritten rule that stopping violence and chucking out the offenders was the steward's job. If the blokes involved were big guys, or if there were more than two fighting, Thomas would approach them with the wooden mallet he used for tapping and spiling the barrels, but usually - if they did not go quietly - he just punched them once or twice with his huge fists and that was the end of the matter. But to David in his bedroom, unable to see that most men in these brawls actively hope for someone to come along and break up what they have drunkenly started before any serious damage is done, his father's presence in the midst of what seemed like unbridled violence filled him with a dreadful fear.

It occurred to David that his father no longer had the sheer physical presence that had formerly allowed him to sort out trouble. Fortunately, there was very little fighting in the club now for his father had soon built a reputation of standing no nonsense and most of the troublemakers had either gone elsewhere to drink or did not fancy another right hook from the man who normally served them behind the bar with more agreeable products. He seemed smaller somehow, thought David, as if his father were slowly collapsing in on himself. And his coughing had got worse, he concluded.

Thomas Rhys had had a bad chest ever since David could remember. The dust, which lined his lungs like malignant black pockets of decay, was a common legacy in the mining valleys. Lately, the bouts of coughing had grown in severity and Thomas had assured David it was just a touch of flu, but this new intensity of coughing had gone on too long for it to be that. Getting him to go to the doctor would be the devil's own job. Eight years ago Thomas had had bronchitis. He struggled against it for days but eventually had to take to his bed in an unheated room in the middle of winter. Pat had taken over most of the work until he got better, but she couldn't manage the barrels in the cellar. David was too small to shift them and no one in the club volunteered to help, so Thomas had to get up and do it himself. As the memory of that day returned to David it seemed to stab through him like a cold blade. He could picture his father dressed in his old army great coat crouched in the cellar readying himself to lift one of the wooden casks and move it out of the way. The effort had seemed enormous to David. Four, five, more times he had done this, and after each lift he sat on the edge of one of the shelves and his whole body had been racked by paroxysms of coughing. His brow had become wreathed in sweat and his arms visibly trembled. When he had finished this work he made his way slowly along the passageway towards David and, as much to comfort his son as to hold himself steady, he had placed his arm around the boy's shoulders and had returned to his bed exhausted. Some of the pain of that moment surfaced again in David when he realized with horror that his father's coughing was becoming more and more like those violent eruptions he had witnessed that day in the cellar.

David felt as if the world he and his family lived in were now approaching some unknown but forbidding edge. He did not fully understand why but he knew it was important not to go over. It was no good simply keeping your head down and hoping for the best; you had to fight if you wanted to stay away from the precipice. A sense of shame gripped him that in recent years he had been too busy with his mates to see what was happening to his own mam and dad. He hadn't meant to be selfish but he had rather taken them for granted while he was out seeing the films, knocking back the drinks, and having the girls that all seemed to come naturally enough to a young man with a bit of money in his pocket. Now David was beginning to see life in Riverside, and the club in particular, in a different light. He decided that he would do whatever he could to keep them all away from the edge.

With this resolution in mind, David left the abandoned mangle and picked a path between the rounded hills where he noticed that some of the ponds in the hollows were now unmistakably fouled with oil; soon not even the newts would be able to live there. As he drew closer to the river itself, thinking of the various ways in which he could help his father in the club, he caught sight of some movement in the tall reeds that grew along this part of the embankment. It was Elaine whose short skirt and bare legs clearly highlighted the patches of mud on her knees. Behind her emerged Cavie who was taken aback when he saw David. Quickly, however, Cavie's look of surprise was replaced by one of hostility, which gave some semblance of animation to his otherwise pimply and sagging face. Then he turned aside and in a little while Elaine followed after him. No more than ten minutes later David had almost reached his home when he saw Flo Roberts, in the house opposite, bring out her old wicker stool and take up her position outside her front door from where she could survey the whole street. He ducked inside the alleyway quickly; he did not want Flo asking him if he'd seen her daughter, Elaine.

Flo was the wrong side of thirty, big, with dark tangled hair, eye lashes heavy with mascara, and thick blotchy hands. It was possible perhaps to be a prostitute in Riverside for nearly twenty years, as had Flo, and still retain some of the physical charms that young and sober men would still lust after, but you wouldn't want to bet on it. If Flo had ever been attractive, it was difficult to see how. None of her children took after her in looks, particularly Elaine who was tomboyish and had a soft, smooth face with penetrating blue eyes. Flo was blowsy and had never made a good living as a pro. Mind you, her kids did not lack for clothes at Whitsuntide when on the Sunday all the children would dress up and parade down the street in their finest. Elaine always looked the prettiest. Her plaited fair hair would swing down over her embroidered dress as she skipped along the pavement, her thin waist shown off by a pink bow. Last Whitsun, however, Elaine had scorned the little-girl-look and had defiantly worn jeans and a tight pullover. But even that attire currently outshone Flo's who, with rolled-down-stockinged feet firmly planted on the pavement outside her door, was now flicking fag ash from the folds of her shapeless mauve dress and watching the movements around her.

Flo wasn't just any bulky woman sat in the sun by her front doorstep. Oh no. This was the legendary local prostitute, who if she showed no inclinations at all towards possessing a heart of gold, at least amused her neighbours with other characteristics. Stories were legion of her drinking some unsuspecting stranger under the table in a pub - she wasn't allowed in any of the clubs - and then making off with his wallet. Likewise, people rejoiced in her complete and utter disregard for the forces of law and order in the shape of the local coppers. There was many a young bobby who had cause to regret a run-in with Flo. But she had other characteristics too that instead of amusing her neighbours sometimes intimidated them. For instance, when the Queen was on her throne by her front door, you couldn't just walk past her. You had to say something to her in a civil fashion for one of Flo's self-evident truths - almost religious was the fervour in which she held it - was that she was as good as the next person. You looked down on her at your peril. Men were required to say nothing more than 'Morning missus' or even to nod politely with a hint of a smile on their faces. Women were expected to ask after her, to pass a comment on the state of the weather, and to provide any information they might have on the whereabouts of her offspring and what they were up to. Any perceived slight might well be met with a hail of abuse, and several people had been physically knocked down by swinging blows from her meaty forearms.

Flo's own mother was still alive, though now quite elderly. Gran Roberts, as everyone called her, had lived nowhere else but Granall Street. She had buried all her brothers and sisters and her husband, whom the neighbours said never got over the shame of his daughter becoming a prostitute. Elaine was devoted to her grandmother and as she grew up, she saw more of her than of Flo who would be out most nights and who sometimes stayed away for days on end. Elaine had started to skip school and while Gran Roberts had spoken quietly to her and tried to make her see sense, Flo felt powerless to intervene. She didn't really know how to talk to her daughter any more than she knew who the father was.

CHAPTER FOUR

It was still warm for late September but as David interrupted his journey briefly to look back towards the jetty, he saw the early morning tide swathed in mist, which obscured the concrete pylons of the suspension bridge so that the roadway seemed to hang in the air unattached to the ground. Until the sun burnt it off the mist covered the churning of the waters by the Rush, but its slightly muffled roar could still be heard even by the abandoned sandpits.

David left the dirt track and soon reached the dole office where he stood silently in the queue behind Plod and waited for it to open. The lines of men had grown steadily longer since the closure of the steelworks and among what had become a fraternity of the dispossessed, there was much anger at the non-appearance of the jobs that had been promised to replace those at the Sceptre plant.

-You can never trust those Tory bastards, said one face in the queue to his neighbour.

-You can't trust any of them, came the reply.

Plod shifted uncomfortably in front of David. It was not the political opinions that upset Plod - what did he care for the likes of all politicians? They were only in it for what they could get; they did fuck all for him. It was the sudden appearance of two plain-clothes policemen, known to Plod from earlier encounters, that had got him worried. They were hanging about opposite the dole queue by the gents toilets. David also saw them and he too recognized them as police officers. They weren't proper CID but uniformed constables on a plain-clothes job who had taken off their jackets and ties, and their helmets, and had donned ordinary overcoats. But the big black boots and the blue serge trousers were still all too evident. They feigned indifference but they were obviously interested in something close by. Immediately, David thought of the recent weeks in which he had been helping his father in the cellar and even serving behind the bar on several nights.

Since David's evening work replaced the hours normally put in by the regular barmaid, who had packed up the job to join a local taxi firm as a radio dispatcher, the committee actually paid David a few pounds. People had got shopped to the dole office for less than that, but David recalled that they usually sent their own people to go snooping around rather than involve the police.

Perhaps the coppers were out to get the gays who frequented the toilets, thought David. But it was too early for that kind of going-on, even for the most excessive satyr. The boys in blue opposite watching the line of men outside the dole office might well have been previously involved in moral crusades - sticking their heads under bog doors to catch people doing things that were none of their business and a complete waste of police time and energy to boot - but they weren't there now for such jolly pastimes.

Plod knew, however, why they were there. He could sense the officers' eyes on the back of his head with almost as much intensity as he could imagine their desire to feel his collar. And feel his collar they would, he thought; and, damn the swines, this time they'd find the fucking watches on him in his pocket. He wondered whether to make a run for it, so he looked around as casually as he could to see what the two officers were doing. They had gone. Plod looked away and was just about to bolt when two sets of heavy black boots and blue serge trousers appeared in front of his gaze. David was surprised at how quietly Plod went; he had a reputation for being hard, and had been to a variety of approved schools and borstals. You had to be careful how you looked at him even. The normally buoyant Plod with his usual stream of obscenities when talking to or about a copper had been led off meekly looking pale and worried.

At the station the two policemen roughly pushed Plod into a cell and slammed the door.

-Now you're going to get what we promised you the last time we met sonny, said one of the officers through the inspection hole.

He was left on his own for the next three hours. The police had searched him earlier and found the watches, so Plod knew they could do him for the break-in or for receiving. Either way they had enough to fix him up - just like they had threatened the last time he had been caught. Only he was a juvenile then and being locked away with a bunch of kids held no terrors. In any event he'd got a fine for the last lot, something he knew really got up the noses of the coppers. They were going to put him away this time and it would be prison. The thought made him shiver involuntarily. The first time he had ever been given a custodial sentence, he'd left the juvenile court feeling like a fucking hero going off to war. But he cried his guts out that night in the cold lock-up. To his surprise, the next morning a quietly spoken man addressed him civilly and told him they were going to help him. When he got over the shock, he knew that being locked up there was going to be piss easy, and a few months later he returned home indeed a hero in the eyes of those boys who had not yet been put away. By the time he went to borstal Plod knew the system. But prison, that was different; there if you showed the slightest weakness, Plod told himself, you were done for. He wasn't at all sure he could face being banged up in prison.

Suddenly the cell door was flung open and a posse of men rushed in. Within a few minutes they had beaten the shit out of Plod who, in the eyes of his assailants, was being paid back for all the times he'd been a disrespectful bastard, for all the occasions he'd gloated at the stupid coppers trying to find the evidence for crimes they were sure he had committed, for being a smart fucker once too often. They left him to grovel in his own blood and later Plod was charged with burglary and with assaulting a police officer in the course of his duty. Later still he was given a small bowl of cold water and a rag with which to clean himself up, and he was held overnight without his clothes to appear before the beak the following day. During the early hours of the morning, as Plod lay on the hard cot shivering and trying to cover his nakedness, the cell door was opened again.

-No more please! No more please God! he cried as he saw the two men enter.

-Sit up! ordered the taller of the two gruffly.

-And make sure you bloody well pay attention laddie, said the other. We have a little proposition for you. Listen up!

The two officers spelled out their proposition in language Plod could understand. There was much talk of scratching backs and of doing one another favours. Plod gave the police what they wanted and they returned his clothes. Soon after this little chat a dawn raid, in which a number of police dogs were given a good healthy work-out, was mounted on the home of an unsuspecting fence, and when Plod appeared later in the court the assault charge against him was dropped. There was no police opposition to bail and Plod was hopeful that at his eventual trial the prison sentence would be suspended, as he had been led to expect. He walked back to Ribley Street - avoiding the river where his mates had met that morning to build a bonfire - and he tried to concoct a good story to explain his bruises. He wondered too where he could get any money for this week now that he had been so rudely prevented from signing on.

In Plod's absence Stomper had assumed command. Judging by the amount of wood collected on the grass embankment, Stomper could see that the bonfire was going to be nowhere near the size of the ones earlier in the year despite the fact that they had all been busy since early morning. He barked out further orders to the younger boys to redouble their efforts to find more wood, and he was immensely pleased to see them head off under the naked glare of the afternoon sun in the direction of the hitherto unexplored Brownhills. Three boys informed him, with a fine sense of the importance of their mission, that they were setting off to the abandoned sand yards some way upstream to fetch an old sofa, which had been left high and dry in one of the sand pits yesterday. When Stomper was satisfied that everyone was gainfully employed in trying to build the biggest bonfire the old landing stage had seen in years, he turned to Cavie and asked his thick-set companion if he would fetch some petrol so that he could be sure to get the fire going.

-Never needed petrol before, said Cavie sullenly.

-We've never had a bonfire so late in the summer before either. Besides, you can see for yourself can't you that a lot of the wood's wet.

There was something defiant in the way that Cavie looked at the handsome features of Stomper, as if he had not yet agreed that in the unexplained absence of Plod he was to take orders from another.

-Let's wait and see what Plod says, Cavie answered.

-Won't matter what he says. With wet wood you'll still need petrol to get it going, said Stomper confidently. Look, you don't have to get it now. Later will do, so long as it's yere when we light the fire tonight, he conceded eventually.

-Righto, said Cavie who thought that by then Plod would have turned up anyway.

Then the two of them silently set to building the bonfire. They dragged the largest pieces of wood into a pile together - luckily part of a tree stump had been washed up and this formed a perfect centre. A boy came back with an armful of drift wood. Stomper thought about the sofa and sent the boy off to find out if it were on its way. In a short while the lad returned all breathless to inform Stomper that his three friends were at that very moment struggling with it along the track just by the power-station. Stomper immediately sent him back again to help carry it. Leaving a space where the sofa would go, he and Cavie proceeded to build up the other side of the bonfire with the medium-sized pieces of wood. With the arrival of the sofa they did the same on the opposite side, and then filled in as many of the gaps as possible with the smallest pieces of drift wood, which the small army of returning boys brought to the site.

It was late afternoon before the job was finished and the bonfire looked large enough to merit (perhaps) the label of being the summer's biggest. The fire would not be lit until after dark and one by one all the boys had drifted home with the intention of returning later. Only Stomper and Cavie remained on guard duty to ensure no gang of spoil-sports from across the river came and destroyed their work.

-You bringing anyone tonight? asked Stomper.

-Doubt it, replied Cavie who was immediately tense and wary.

-Oh, I thought you might have been with that bint... Elaine.

-What gives you that idea? asked Cavie.

-You've been giving her one, haven't you? said Stomper in a tone more accusatory than complimentary.

Cavie's eyes burnt with anger. All the resentment he felt towards the preening Stomper with his sarky comments and ever-so-clever put-downs was released within Cavie with the energy of an explosion. He grasped Stomper around the throat with both hands and pressed home his attack viciously.

-You've got a big mouth, d'you know that Stomper, a big mouth. Now just shut up about her!

Cavie gripped Stomper even more tightly as his opponent began to struggle.

-Lay off you crazy fucker! said Stomper with some difficulty under the pressure being exerted on his throat.

Although much lighter than his adversary Stomper managed to snap Cavie's head back sharply with a punch, but he was unable to loosen his frenzied grip. Stomper threw more punches - some of which missed and those blows that hit the target had little effect - and then he tried to twist his body around in yet another attempt to break the painful hold on his neck.

-Let go you bastard! he croaked.

But Cavie was suffused with a volcanic anger to the extent that he did not hear his friend's cries nor feel any of the increasingly feeble blows that landed on his head. With one final effort of will, Stomper drew Cavie closer to him and then with all the force he could muster he drove his knee deep into Cavie's groin. Immediately his opponent screamed, released his grip, and fell to his knees on the muddy ground. No sooner had he fallen than Stomper kicked Cavie full in the face and then, as Cavie rolled over under the force of the blow, Stomper brought his heel down hard once more into his balls for good measure. Stomper gasped for air as he staggered back a few paces; Cavie lay on the ground and gently rocked back and forth on his side with his knees drawn up to his chest. He was crying very quietly.

-You fucking mad bastard! So you're knocking some jailbait tart. So what? Is that any reason to go fucking ape? Stomper asked when he had recovered sufficient breath.

Cavie wanted to stand up, to tell him it wasn't like that. But, in truth, he didn't want to have to tell him anything. It was none of Stomper's damn business what he and Elaine did. It was best to keep it quiet and not have people like him shooting his mouth off. If Cavie said he was screwing a fourteen-year-old, the other boys would jeer at him and ask why couldn't he get a real woman, not some tart of a girl. And if he said he wasn't poking her, they'd jeer all the more and say why ever fucking not. Can't you get inside even a little tart's knickers who's probably begging for it? No, Cavie didn't want to tell Stomper or anyone else anything about it, not least what he and Elaine had really been doing. So he lay there in the mud, said nothing, and tried to think of the pain going away.

-Fuck you then! shouted Stomper who promptly turned away and made off.

An hour later Cavie was found by Plod. He had eventually emerged from his house and, having heard from one of the young boys that the bonfire was ready but needed petrol to set it blazing, had come to the riverbank to inspect the work.

-What the fuck happened? asked Plod.

-I could say the same to you, said Cavie looking at Plod's bruised face.

-It's nothing, insisted Plod with some force. I just had a bust-up with the coppers, that's all. What about you? What the hell's going on?

-I was riding one of the kids' bikes up on the track when I lost control and crashed down yere, lied Cavie.

He saw Plod looking around.

-The little sod just picked up his bike and buggered off leaving me, said Cavie rather too quickly.

-Well, d'you want me to get you back home or what?

-No thanks, said Cavie. It'll be time soon to light the fire. I'll stay yere. It's the biggest bonfire we've ever built, don't you think?

-The last one was much bigger, said Plod dismissively.

Between the unyielding solidity of the terraced streets and the grey swollen waters of the river ran the cratered dirt track along which, at twilight, the youngsters made their way towards the bonfire. For as long as anyone could recall, this track had led the children from the commonplaces of their tarmac streets to the dangerous but desirable location of treacherous mud and swift tides. It urged older boys and men, still faithful to their acquired skills of fishing, to tramp eagerly towards some trusty spot to seek out the crevices of eels. It allowed old men to pass, just barely; it even allowed them to reach a rusted bench near the landing stage where they could sit and remember their youth that had ebbed away. All told, it was a busy if neglected highway frequently commandeered by children, fishermen, and dog owners exercising their pets, and sometimes it was used by women too, though they were usually looking for kids, husbands, or dogs. The river seemed to beckon all things and, if you gave it the chance or were careless, it would consume them too.

The Effyl was still rising and most of the youngsters had gathered around the still unlit bonfire when an effervescent speed boat appeared in the middle of the channel. It clawed its way downstream against the impregnated tide only veering from its central path to allow a ponderous sand boat to pass as it hoved into view around the bend by the ship scrapyards. Few of the children bothered to study the speed boat, which was altogether out of place; but the sand boat always drew admiring attention. It was something to do with the patience with which the black-painted vessel used the very power of the river to reach its berth. She would slide along slowly with the tide, her heavily laden flanks low down in the water, until she was a little way upstream of the wharf on the far bank where she was unloaded and where the sand stood in pyramidal piles awaiting the lorries to cart it off to building sites. Having reached the precise spot upriver, she would drop anchor and allow the tide to sweep her around in a majestic arc, her stern sometimes scooping out swathes of soft mud from the sloping flanks of the river closest to the embankment, after which she would raise anchor and nudge gently forwards and sidewards into dock.

As the tide licked the last jagged edges of the grassy embankment, like some grotesque fringe in a half-remembered nightmare, the bonfire (after much petrol had been used) was kick-started into life by Plod who, though he had taken no part in its construction, insisted on setting it alight. Everyone stood as close as he or she could and stared into the flames, which shot up into the clear and newly darkened sky. Several children poked long branches into the fire and when they had them alight, they carried them like torches and climbed over the landing stage as if they were explorers finding some great ruin in the dark jungle. The men on the bow of the sand boat, which had silently drawn level with the fire, could be seen waving and all the children shouted and waved back. The older boys offered cigarettes to the teenage girls, and Plod himself opened a bottle of vodka and passed it to his chosen few. Some of the youths had come with swimming costumes beneath their jeans and they were already sliding down the muddy flanks of the river into the water. After swimming briefly in the river - close to the waterline - they clambered back to the embankment with their legs and arms sinking deeply into the mud which, as they warmed themselves by the fire, hardened into a solid cake so that they looked as if they had been prepared for a pagan ritual.

Then, notwithstanding their strange appearance, the youths chased the girls around the fire and if they caught one they would try to steal a kiss, but most of the girls screeched and pushed them away and complained of the flakes of mud messing their skirts. This made some of the boys run again to the flanks of the river, slowly being uncovered more and more by the now retreating tide, and scoop up handfuls of wet mud with which to threaten the pieces of skirt. Faced with a couple of lads holding their arms out wide with their palms full of dripping mud, the girls ran off into the gloom away from the fire until the boys thought better of the prank and slid down the mud valleys again into the water. There the youths tried to turn handstands in the soft yielding ooze, which made the returning girls laugh out loud at their antics. The laughter rose to a crescendo and then was halted by the rattle of the sand boat's anchor as it dropped towards the water. The heavy anchor splashed into the river and was carried away by the current, and everyone's attention was drawn upstream to watch the vessel's stately progress. It was while all heads were turned towards the boat that Stomper arrived at the bonfire carrying reinforcements of strong liquor. With him was Elaine.

Even Plod, who was by then more than half-cut, could sense the naked hatred in the gaze that Cavie turned on Stomper. So that's how he got all marked up, thought Plod with some surprise. The sand boat had docked and some of the younger children, who remembered the dire threats issued to them about what time they had to be in, were reluctantly returning home to bed. The fire was beginning to die down so that the first leaps over it - complete with loud whoops and yells - had already been ventured. Cavie ignored the others; he failed even to look in Elaine's direction who had sat a little way from the fire and was sipping from a bottle Stomper had given her. Cavie's gaze and thoughts were centred entirely on Stomper - the lean Stomper who was stripping off to his costume in the warm light of the fire; the handsome Stomper who was athletically climbing to the top of the landing stage; the confident Stomper who dived so assuredly into the half-gloom of the water below the jetty and who emerged so freely to swim back to shore; the swaggering Stomper who returned to drink in long gulps from the same bottle as Elaine; and, finally, the intimate Stomper who pressed his thighs against Elaine's face who turned and kissed the glistening wetness.

Before Cavie could channel the hatred within him, which momentarily rooted him to the spot - Stomper must now know about him and Elaine, he feared - and before he could hurl himself upon his foe, Stomper ran towards the landing stage and began to climb it again, this time a little less assuredly as the alcohol dulled his agility. The flickering light from the bonfire fell on Stomper for a moment as he stood perfectly still on the edge of the jetty. Twenty feet below were the dark waters of the Effyl. Stomper's face was aglow with a sense of pride - he was above them all; he had built the biggest bonfire seen for ages; he had taken Cavie's girl; and he had the attention right now of the whole fucking world. Even Plod would have to look out in future, he thought.

He steadied himself and then drew his body up onto his toes and held his arms out in front of him. With a deft bend of the knees, Stomper leapt into space. There was such a vigour and a majesty about his high, graceful leap that he seemed for the barest second to hang motionless in the air. He was smiling. Suddenly, there was a terrible roar as the Rush opened up. Countless gallons of water instantly spewed out of the huge pipes into the river so that the area around the jetty exploded into a violent nightmare of turbulence. The cries of the small crowd on the embankment were lost in the harsh drumming of the Rush, as too was the scream on the lips of Stomper as he dived headlong into the maelstrom. The last thing that Cavie saw of Stomper was the horror scribbled quickly across his face before he disappeared into the vortex. The throes and hideous palpitations of the Rush held Stomper under and repeatedly smashed his body against the piles of the jetty. Then, with throbbing ferocity, the Rush dragged him along the concrete slipway, still under the grey Effyl, before it allowed him to pop up like a ragdoll further downstream. Stomper's lifeless body floated off unseen in the darkness beyond the warm glow of the bonfire. Some turds from the sewer bobbed around it and, for a short distance, kept the body company. Those still left on the bank were at first speechless; then a few began to sob hysterically while Plod and the older boys ran to the water's edge and called Stomper's name repeatedly.

They found Stomper's body the next morning on the far bank two miles downstream. You would never have thought he'd been a handsome lad.

CHAPTER FIVE

Three weeks after Stomper had been buried the flowers, still inside their cellophane wrappers strewn across the grave, had withered away and the stalks had become sodden. His mother was the only one who went to see him now. On one occasion she thought she had seen a thin fair-haired girl near her son's grave, but the girl had made off before she got close enough to be sure. The verdict on Steven Price, Stomper, had been death by misadventure. At first, Mrs. Price's grief had been mingled with bitterness that her lad had been so cruelly taken away. But now she had found solace in religion, which had always been in the background of her life waiting for the time to reassert itself. Accordingly, in this new state of awareness, she did not blame God for her loss, but asked Him to watch over her son and to guard him from all evil in the safe bosom of heaven. During her prayers she would kneel by the side of Stomper's grave, the mound of brown earth and yellow clay still settling back, and earnestly beg God to receive her son's soul. Wrapped up in an old woollen coat whose hem soaked up the muddy water as she knelt, and with a faded headscarf tied tightly under her chin, she looked a comic supplicant. Not because she loved her son, but because she still believed in a god.

There was a beautiful futility about her performance. The sentiments of her simple prayer could do no more than mingle mockingly with the squelch of the rain as it fell into the nearby puddles surrounding the grave. Her words could only hang about her in the nebulous air until, finally, their cruel echo faded and died. Her devotions were like a straw as she went through her own version of drowning - drowning in sorrow for what could no longer be. Ironically, Stomper himself would have found the whole idea a real laugh, for he had known even in so short a life that prayers altered nothing in Riverside.

Throughout the narrow claustrophobic length of Granall and Ribley streets there was now a sombre mood. It had nothing to do with

Stomper's death; rather it was the result of the autumn mists that often snaked down from the river at this time of year. At such moments, Ribley Street in particular seemed partially to dissolve into this grey yielding shroud, but never so much that its slow deterioration became completely masked. In all the streets in Riverside there was a sense of people and things being worn away. It wasn't just the crumbling bricks, the rotting window frames, and the missing roof slates. Inside the houses the faded curtains, worn lino, and battered pots and pans all added to the physical dilapidation. But the decay was more than physical, it was something that touched people's souls; not the souls they think they must dedicate to God, but their own human spirit. Here in Riverside many spirits were in decline. There was too much making do, too much scrimping and saving, so that it became an expected way of life. Often it was a matter of recycling what you had as best you could, until ideas about getting your head above water and becoming a little better off seemed like cruel and vindictive shibboleths. People outside Riverside expected the inhabitants of these streets to get on, but such uninformed judges had little idea how difficult it was simply to survive.

David emerged from the alleyway into Granall Street. He was still sweating slightly from his work in the cellar and the dank air made him shiver. He was on his way to town to buy a record that had taken his fancy on the radio. Opposite, the beaded curtain across the open front door of Elaine's house hung silently. There was no wicker stool by the door for Flo was still in bed. The man who had come back with her last night had left immediately after finishing his business on Flo's bed, and the seepage of his semen had soaked into the crumpled sheet on which Flo was sleeping and had left a circular yellowish stain. There were other, fainter, stains on the sheet, and these were made by different men who had in common only that they had each paid extra to ride Flo bareback without the encumbrance of a johnny.

When Elaine had been younger, Gran Roberts had tried to shield her from the full knowledge of her mother's activities. If Flo's half-stifled moans - a necessary accompaniment for the majority of punters - had woken Elaine, her grandmother would go into Elaine's room and read her fairy tales until she fell asleep once again. If Flo brought a man home during the day Gran Roberts would give Elaine a few pence and send her outside to buy sweets and to play with her friends. But, of course, Elaine soon clicked to what was going on. Her first reaction as a child had been to fly at anyone who taunted her and called her mother a slag. Then, as she became a teenager, she became more detached, only feeling an occasional sense of distaste whenever Flo returned home with a man every bit as fat and drunk as herself. She grew more and more attached to the reassuring figure of the old woman who, in effect, became a substitute for her own mother. For her part, Flo recognized that there was precious little affection between Elaine and herself and was content to let Gran Roberts look after her and the other two children. One of those, another girl, had been taken into care at an early age - it was said Flo's neighbours had complained to the social workers. The other lived at home still but he was a sickly boy not yet of school age and he rarely ventured out. The social workers had their eyes on him too, so it was said, but Elaine was judged too old now to be uprooted.

Old Man Morgan's door was open as David passed and saw him struggling down the stairs carrying a one bar electric fire. David's offer to help was gratefully accepted and as he took the fire into the back room he was surprised to see a bed there.

-I gave a couple of kids a few bob to fetch it down for me, said Old Man Morgan who nodded in the direction of the single divan.

-I'd have done that for you, said David. Why didn't you ask?

-Well, seemed simpler that way and I didn't want to be beholden to anyone.

-Suit yourself, said David but not in an unkindly fashion. Where do you want this fire then Mr. Morgan?

Old Man Morgan pointed to a spot in front of his bed.

-Can't afford the coal anymore so I thought I'd use the electric fire now an' then, he said by way of explanation.

The cable was too short to reach the socket from the position indicated by Old Man Morgan.

-It could go in the corner I suppose. I spends a lot of me time in bed now anyway, Old Man Morgan said with a small sigh.

He did not seem to know where to place his bent frame as David carried the fire around the room to try out several positions. David noticed that the hearth was swept clean; no fire had been lit in it for some while. Behind the door into the scullery hanging on a hook were the old man's bedclothes, his long red dressing gown looking quite resplendent against the chipped and faded paintwork and the patches of damp on the wallpaper. On the tops of a chest of drawers and a heavy mahogany sideboard a layer of dust had gathered undisturbed.

-I could get you some more flex, said David.

Old Man Morgan seemed to stiffen slightly but he relaxed when he was assured that it was just an old piece of cable laying around the club that would be thrown out sooner or later.

-I'll bring it later on, and I'll fix it all up for you if you like, David offered.

-That would be good of you lad. My hands shake a little too much now for me to make the join.

Old Man Morgan looked fondly at the youngster before him and he imagined himself briefly to be no longer in his worn-out scullery with David; he was off elsewhere in the company of other young men, in another time, where he was no longer old. And then the knowledge of his increasing incapacity recaptured his thoughts and the tears forming in his eyes told him differently - he was old after all.

-Aye, righto then lad, he said turning away as quickly as he could to hide his face from David. See you later on then, is it?

David stepped out of the house into Granall Street and wondered if life had a lonely old age waiting for him too. His gaze was drawn back up the street by the emergence of Gran Roberts with her mop and bucket of water through the beaded curtain by her door. She set to cleaning the cracked and uneven pavement in front of the house. As if a signal had been communicated to all the women in the street, suddenly other mops and pails were in evidence scattered along the terrace. Some of the older women were still in the habit of blacking their doorsteps and their old fireside hobs. But however hard they worked they could not repair the loose paving slabs, which shot water up the back of your leg when you trod on them during a rainy day, nor could they erase the dirt between the slabs, which seemed to replenish itself with ease. And, of course, they were powerless against the oppressive smells of the glue factory.

The pavement in Granall Street was nothing more than an interlocking mosaic of cracks, while the road surface was a mixture of grey chippings and bald patches of tar on which were flattened the pink chewed-to-death castaways of bubble-gum. Children playing games constantly discarded their gum as they ran helter-skelter along the street and the gum was now so ground into the surface that the little pink splodges had become a permanent part of the road. Certainly, little traffic went down Granall Street to wear them away. The street remained a thoroughfare claimed, for the most part, by people rather than cars. Middle-aged men still decked themselves out on their doorsteps, guts overflowing thick leather belts or wearing bracers like harnesses, and faces weathered and full of spiky whiskers - the kind of men who picked up grandchildren with an 'oopsadaisy' and drew their bristles across soft pink faces so that they made red patches on the children's cheeks like the curse of their own wasted lives, the mark of Riverside, a river pox. It was a street full of aprons and home perms nodding to one another across the way, of heated curlers turned up to heaven to divine the weather, and of thin female lips shouting first at streaky-legged Janice to get away from that bloody scarlet-fever-infested drain and to stop picking her nose, and then at Bert to get up for his dinner. And then one of the women with a perm would engage another on the topic of how kids can be such beggars, and Janice would just miss a clout as she asked for some money to buy sweets, and Bert would shout for something to eat. The thin-lipped woman would return to the room of Bert-demand and the others would go in search of another vacant window sill and another vacant conversation.

The young men and women would treat the street as their own on their return late at night from a good time up town. Often the young men would hang around at the top of the road by the junction with Dankley Alley and they would finish off the last cans of beer and extol the virtues of Susan, Tricia, and all the others. The alcohol and the desire to impress pals would drive at least one of them to graphic descriptions of recent conquests. The account was always given in a voice at times clamorous and boastful, and at others almost in a whisper while friends were vouchsafed the most salacious details as if they were co-conspirators. People already in bed in their houses nearby thus heard only snatches of the tale - tits as big as this (with hand movements); rubbed her all over; sucked me like there was no tomorrow; all the way in; shot my load.

But it was the children above all others who owned the street. Along Granall Street, at the appropriate times of the year, you could find Cardiff Arms Park, Wembley Stadium, Lords, and even Wimbledon though few children owned a tennis racket, using instead their hands or a roughly shaped piece of chipboard to hit the ball over an imaginary net. The classic games of sport were always played on the grand scale with the children taking on the personae of the heroes of the day. There were local traditions too, such as 'Long Lamp' and 'Yallaco', communal games in which a good turn of speed and an ability to dodge one's pursuers were of the essence. The boys and girls of Granall Street and the Riverside area passed their childhood years in good spirits and companionship, until the time came for a different kind of solidarity as they started their first shifts and they experienced their first taste of boredom or of grime and oil rubbed into their flesh. Another worker would then take his or her place in Riverside, another person with a poor old age to look forward to.

There were old people in the street too, but many were now so infirm that to put in an appearance outside their homes was beyond them. Some lived alone as best they could with occasional help from the welfare. When they could cope no longer, they were taken away and put in a home and forgotten. When they died a big black hearse, its paintwork long dulled by the sulphurous air, came and took them away; then they were put in the ground like pink bubble-gum stuck to the guts of the earth, used up, sapped, and discarded. The infirm who lived still with relatives were shielded from the excesses of their own mortality as best could be achieved by being tucked up in curtained box rooms, full of the odour of medicine and warm sweaty blankets, with the lingering hopes of recoveries that rarely ever came. The other elderly - those who could still move themselves or be moved without too much bother - were often to be glimpsed just inside a hallway or, when the weather was really warm, on a doorstep. Clad in ill-assorted garments and full of tumours and ancient warts, they sat precariously on their chairs and waited for the dull black cars to take them away.

At the top of the street as David turned into Dankley Alley and was about to cross the road he almost stepped on a pigeon cowering in the gutter. Its left leg was twisted and limp and a length of fishing gut was tightly tangled around the now useless limb and around its wing. Fifty yards away three small boys were laying the same trap for some other pigeon, all but ignoring Peety Malone who was watching their preparations intently. The boys paid out some line in a circle inside which they placed a few pieces of bread. The circle was really a noose however, and one of the boys held the end of the line ready to snap it shut when a pigeon walked into the trap. The trick rarely worked first time, but that was no problem since pigeons were stupid birds. Even though they had escaped the noose previously, the pigeons actually sat on the roofs and watched the trap being prepared and baited afresh, and when it was finished they would fly down and give the boys another chance.

The bird before David now had given them one chance too many and it would obviously be finished off by a cat soon. Mary O'Flaherty and Betty Sawyer were returning from the shops and discussing the previous night's winner of the club jackpot when they saw David pick up the stricken pigeon.

-The poor thing, said Betty in her warm-hearted way. P'raps I could take it home till it's better.

-Don't talk so bloody silly Betty, said Mary who was sentimental about nothing and nobody.

-What are you going to do with it? Betty forced herself to ask.

-He's going to wring its bloody neck. Aren't you luv? cut in Mary.

-It's the best way, replied David to Betty's question.

-Oh! I can't watch. C'mon Mary let's be off down the club.

-I'm right behind you me old lovely, Mary assured her.

-Peety! You get away from those other boys now, do you hear me? shouted Betty before she picked up her shopping and carried on her way.

David could feel the bird's heart beating frantically. A faint musty smell reached his nostrils, and his fingers - wrapped gently around the pigeon - felt as if they had become impregnated with a film of grease. He removed one hand from the bird's body and with it he took a firm grip on the creature's neck. He twisted the neck quickly and threw the dead bird into a nearby dustbin where it lay limp and contorted.

On his way to the track by the river David saw Cavie who was walking up Ribley Street. Cavie had taken to hanging about with a few lads in Dankley Alley, but his attention always seemed to be on Granall Street, which he watched like a hawk to see if Elaine had come out of her house. Sometimes he would go down Granall Street to talk to Elaine but he could never get her on her own. Of Plod little had been seen since Stomper's death, but there was a rumour among the lads of his age that he was staying low because he was scared of the police.

David felt good to have left the street behind. The tide was very low and it was a long way down the flanks of the river to the water. It gave David a feeling of space and of escape from the constricting terraced houses and the narrow alleyways and roads. As he passed the dole office he was surprised to see the treasurer of the Coronation Road Working Men's Club going inside. David had no idea that Tony Newbold had also lost his job like so many others in Riverside, but he supposed it wouldn't make that much difference to the club. As David made his way towards Smiths in the centre of town to buy his record, he suddenly felt an urgent need to relieve himself. The gents by the dole office weren't far away, but the thought that a ridiculous copper might be poking around inside the bog looking for wayward pricks rather put him off. He decided instead, since he was fairly presentably dressed, to dash across the road into the posh Kings Head Hotel.

The foyer of the hotel was all chrome and mirrors, and angular young men in dark suits behind the smart reception desk seemed to be eyeing David as he stood in the middle of the deep pile carpet desperately searching for the toilets. A porter with a bright red cummerbund, which to David made him look a right prat, came over and said in a hoity-toity voice that was not his normal tone if he could help sir in any way. David asked for the gents and was pointed in their direction with a theatrical sweep of the porter's hand. David worried whether you tipped people in these places for such services.

Inside the gentlemen's toilet there was more chrome and mirrors, and also clear glass splash panels in front of the capacious urinals. David wondered just how daft these rich bastards must be that they needed such space and precautions in order not to piss down their own trouser legs and all over their poncey patent leather shoes. Before he had time to pursue this line of thought, and barely before he had shaken his cock and put it away, the toilet door opened and the obsequious porter appeared; David recognized he had outlived his welcome. You needed money, he thought, and to flash it around to be welcomed and to feel at ease in an expensive hotel like this. Outside a big car was dropping off guests at the hotel. It was one of those vehicles that had soft carpets that seemed to wrap right around you as you sat in the back and sank into the leather seats. David had never been in one; not even the black hearse that came to the street was as posh as this car. Both the car and the hotel appeared strangely out of place. Only a few yards away were the town centre shops, which unlike the sleek hotel and the fine car, were becoming increasingly dilapidated. A few of the smaller premises, such as long-established traditional tailors, had actually closed as money became tighter. The bigger chain stores had extended their summer sales into late October in an attempt to encourage more people to part with some of their redundancy cash, but business was still lethargic. A once vibrant shopping centre was now sliding towards a depression, which not even the tawdry goods on sale in the shop windows could lift.

Pat Rhys looked about her front room and experienced her own kind of depression. The bottom part of the window had lace curtains drawn across it in time-honoured style, but at the sides were two brightly coloured blinds, which hung down elegantly showing off their pretty pattern. There was a decent bit of carpet on the floor, but Pat could not help reminding herself that neither carpet nor curtains really went very well with the green-upholstered three-piece suite. In fact, it was all a bit too fussy, as far as she was concerned. A nice wallpaper would make all the difference, she convinced herself momentarily before the sight of some of the present paper curling away from the wall dashed her hopes. The bloody damp buggered up everything. She sighed and then asked herself silently why she should bother anyway. They hardly used the front room, she thought, so perhaps she should concentrate on the scullery and see what could be done with that.

She heard Thomas open the door into the scullery - he had come down from the club to make himself another cup of tea before he had to open - and Pat went through to join him. He looked pale as he sat down heavily in his chair by the fire after switching on the electric kettle.

-Sorry luv, I clean forgot about your cuppa, she greeted him.

-No matter. It won't take me a jiffy to make a pot, he answered in his deep voice.

He pushed his hair back into place with a stroke of his fingers and closed his eyes.

-You must be tired, said Pat. Why don't you see the doctor, Tom? Maybe he can give you something to stop you coughing so heavy in the night. You can't be getting enough sleep can you being up half the night?

-Perhaps you're right. I'm sorry Pat, I hadn't meant for you to suffer with me, he said referring to the fact that his bouts also kept Pat awake.

-Oh, don't talk so far back mun! she said with mock severity. It's not me that's suffering; it's you.

The kettle boiled and Pat brewed the tea; Thomas was still slumped in the chair and looking more drained than ever. He had taken lately to falling into a deep sleep in the late afternoon after stop tap, and it was only with great difficulty that Pat could wake him to reopen at six in the evening.

-Listen Tom, she said softly. Maybe David can open up for you. Why don't you get off to bed and have a proper rest?

-The lad's gone up town to buy a record or something, so he said. He'll be back soon enough, and I'll have a breather then.

-Then let me open up for you, urged Pat.

-Thanks all the same, but I've got to check the till readings and adjust the cash before I bank it later, said Thomas trying to perk up a bit.

His wife's anxiety was almost palpable. Thomas rose from the chair and, approaching Pat who was stood by the fire, he put his arm around her slim waist. She seemed to melt within his embrace and, for a brief warm moment, it was as if the cares of the world no longer existed. Fleetingly, before he had to unfold his arm because of another bout of coughing, Pat Rhys felt safe.

Thomas knew what was worrying his wife; it wasn't the state of the wallpaper or the lack of an evening off together any more - though these were important they were almost background concerns. What had caused this onset of acute anxiety was the No.2 account with the brewery. He would do his best to reassure her again that all was well.

-The club takings are down a bit, Thomas began to explain. But it's not drastic and as far as the fiddle is concerned it's only a matter of a couple of bottles of whisky less each week. Anyway, it's not the number of bottles that matters; it's the till accounts. The sums are easy. You know how many measures there are in a bottle of whisky and you know the price of each one, and you also know how many of your own bottles of scotch you've sold in the club in the week. You just multiply the figures together and make sure that the total amount is deducted from the weekly till reading. But you know all this Pat; you know there's no problem.

-I just worry that's all that the committee might decide out of the blue to do another till reading, admitted Pat. They could come along at any time to check the takings.

-They could, but they're too bloody stupid to do it.

-But suppose they did Tom?

-Then they'd think they'd had a good week and I'd be a few pounds out of pocket, wouldn't I?

-Then how could you let the takings drop the following week? It would look funny, suggested Pat.

-Like I said, I'd have to convince them they'd had a one-off week of good trade. Do you remember years ago when I plain forgot to alter the till reading and Tony Newbold turned up at the usual time, and to my horror all my own takings hadn't been deducted? Tony was going on about how pleased the club would be and I had to tell him not to be too quick off the mark. I said the higher-than-normal takings were because I'd returned an awful lot of empties to the brewery and how I'd entered the money on the returns on the till. He and the committee believed it hook, line and sinker, said Thomas with quiet satisfaction.

-But it's not only the whisky Tom. What about the barrels on the No.2 account?

-What about them? Like the whisky you can't tell my barrels from the club's just by looking at 'em, and anyway I've never seen a bloody committee man down the cellar yet in all the years we've been yere. So okay, the stock taker would know, but Jim's no problem and I make sure he gets a little something.

-I don't want you to get careless, said Pat.

-I'm not getting careless and before you say it, I'm not getting greedy either. When the takings drop so does my order to the brewery; when they go back up so will the No. 2 account. Now can we leave it be?

-Just you be careful Thomas Rhys, said Pat. I'll send David up when he's back so you can have a rest. Okay?

-Okay, said Thomas with a tinge of both sadness and resignation. Send the boy along if he's willing.

CHAPTER SIX

It was rumoured that the repair works would soon be laying off men now that there were no more railway wagons going into the Sceptre plant to deliver iron ore, scrap metal, and limestone. In fact, the amount of rail traffic in the Cwmporth area had dropped considerably and unless the repair works could get business elsewhere prospects looked poor. It was always the same: close one huge industrial plant and there are a thousand hemorrhages elsewhere. However, it was Charlie Hawkins's haemorrhoids that bothered him most right now, not the future of the wagon repair works where he was employed. Charlie was trying to twist the top half of his bulky body around so that his podgy arm could more easily reach the crevice of his backside. It was 7.30 am and he was on his way to the toilet cubicles at the end of the engineering shed. So regular and punctual was Charlie's early morning shit that arriving line-managers set their watches by him. In addition to his time-keeping role, Charlie provided a valuable boost to managerial morale for the bosses referred to him among themselves as 'slug'. Had Charlie been asked his preference he would have indicated Mister Hawkins or even Chairman Hawkins, as he was fond of introducing himself when engaged on club business. But the managers had a point; he did move like a slug - slowly and uneventfully as if to move more quickly would be an entirely alien act - and when he went along the shed sweeping up the dust and the shavings from around the lathes you could see where he had been just like a slug leaving a silvery trail.

Charlie sat down inside one of the cubicles, unfurled his cocksucking newspaper, and allowed himself to relax. His heavy jowls fell slack as he eyed the tits on the page in front of him. When he had finished his business and fully appreciated the young lady's assets, he returned to the floor of the engineering shed. Charlie gazed up and down the length of the walkways between the machines with an intimacy bordering on malice. Directly in front of him, leaning in its own personal stupor, was a brush; a brush with long firm bristles, a brush with a once-upon-a-time white shaft, which was now marked with greasy fingerprints; Charlie's brush. He was required for most of his shift - when not cleaning the toilets or personally sitting on one of them - to push this brush around the shed. It was his brush, no one else's, so that it felt at times to Charlie as if it were a physical sign of his incompleteness, like an artificial leg or, worse, an unmentionable stigma that he dragged around with him. There was no joy in sweeping up and no excitement in wielding a brush. Charlie Hawkins was not a romantic man but he had once enjoyed a day dream in which he had fancied himself as a gallant and honourable knight wielding his trusty broad sword in his armoured hands. Then, unbidden by him consciously, the brush had suddenly taken the place of the sword and the heroic tale in which he had imagined himself was transformed into a comic tragedy.

Charlie went through brushes like some of the young blokes told him they went through women. The women were all different, and the brushes were all the fucking same, thought Charlie. Stuff 'em. These young lads were all too cock-happy anyway. Go through women like shelling peas be buggered. Load of bloody bullshit. Did they think he couldn't get it up anymore? Youngsters - what do they fucking know? They should have been on the outing with him, then they would have seen. Christ! He was like a bloody sun god on that trip. Everything revolved around him; he had to organize the people on the buses, sort out the booze - Jesus! he'd put a lot away on the journey down to Barry - and he'd had to tell everyone where to meet and at what time for the leg home. He'd even had to look after Steve Curtice's wife when they had lost one another in the fairground. He'd taken her for a drink and then for a meal in Mitchells cafe near the station. Christ, she was roaring drunk and flirting like a tart too, playing footsies with him under the table as they wolfed their cod and chips. So, he took her round the back of the carpark and had her up against an empty coach. She was all over him, lapping it up she was - these young wankers should have seen him then. Mind she was tight though and he had to push like hell to get inside and she was moaning 'Oh Charlie, don't!', but she wanted it really. Christ! She was begging for it at the end.

One of the bosses shouted across at Charlie who was stood in one of the walkways enjoying his sweet memories of the club outing. He took hold of his brush, its smooth greasy shaft reminded him with a thrill of the way Shirley Curtice had stroked his cock before he thrust into her, but the boss was still watching him and he had to start sweeping. So, he switched off his thoughts and went about his monotonous routine. He was no longer a sun god.

Even in Riverside, factory hooters sounded each day to allow workers to go home, though it sometimes appeared from the bleak look on their faces that they had been consigned to the work place for weeks at a time. Shortly after the shrill whistles had ceased women would swap one place of work for another, and men would all too often expect to be waited on hand and foot. Some men, with sensible wives who would not entirely put up with these expectations, would learn to do something to help about the house, even if it was the women who still carried the biggest load. Other men were either too selfish or too stupid to learn anything, and in their homes the women carried the biggest burdens of all. Few men, however, held to the view that their wives ought to stay more or less permanently indoors, or at least as close to home as domestic duties would allow. So it was that a lot of married women in Riverside had jobs, which were mostly low-paid and part-time, but which brought in much-welcomed and needed cash for all of that.

The wives were often to be seen out with their husbands in the evenings in the local pubs and clubs. Few of the women cared for the pints of bitter enjoyed by their menfolk, but all sorts of ways were found to have a good time and a few drinks. A rough and ready rule associated with having a good time meant husbands and wives often going out together to the same place; but it didn't necessarily mean doing the same things. A lot of clubs had a separate snooker room from which women were excluded. It was not uncommon therefore to see husbands, quite dutiful in their own way, taking drinks to their wives and enquiring of them if the bingo was going well before they retired again into the green baize sanctum. For their part many of the women liked this arrangement and called it 'having a good night out with my husband'.

The Coronation Road Working Men's Club had no snooker room like most of the other clubs in Riverside so it had to evolve another strategy to ensure the separation of the sexes. On Saturday nights if there were a concert or a dance everyone mixed together throughout the whole club. Twice-weekly bingo sessions were the same. The rest of the time there was a form of segregation in which the front (and biggest) part of the club was reserved for men only, and the back part for husbands and wives together and women on their own. This sometimes resulted, if a wife left alone at the back of the club for too long had finished her drink and decided to get another, in a woman arriving at the rear serving hatch of the bar and waving at her husband in an attempt to get him to pay for the order. Some younger women were beginning to object to the way they could be herded around at the convenience of the men. Women had no vote in the club however, so it was a practice that showed signs of being relaxed but not entirely abolished. But when you saw men and women together in the clubs, with their faces intent on their bingo cards or their heads eagerly tilted back to drain their glasses, there did not appear to be any difference at all between them. They were all equally trying to escape for a while the things in Riverside that were oppressive and that held them down.

Thomas Rhys watched the last of the club members making their way home along Coronation Road. A few made a detour into the fish and chip shop opposite, and a young married couple gazed into the window of Healey's and debated which television set they would choose if they had the money. Some of those the worse for wear were having difficulty getting across the road. A passing car sounded its horn angrily but the group made it safely to the other side amidst much laughter and mock fist-shaking at the now long-departed vehicle. Thomas closed and locked the front door of the club and remembered to turn off the illuminated sign outside over the door. As he returned to the bar the air was still heavy with smoke, which wafted in blue-tinged layers towards the ceiling. Pat pulled down one of the shutters at the bar with rather more force than was needed, and the wooden frame shuddered as it hit the counter with a loud bang. The noise made David jump just as he opened the door of the stove to make sure it was dying down nicely for the night.

-I'll do that, said Thomas to his wife as she reached to pull down another shutter, which was code between them for 'just one more round of drinks'.

-It's long past stop tap, protested Pat but without too much force.

She had decided it was probably better not to make a fuss and simply to let the hangers-on and the titty men have their drink. Chairman Hawkins was particularly keen to have another pint of bitter for he had still not slaked the thirst caused by compering that night's concert and by knocking out a few songs. His ridiculous red bow tie was now stuffed inside his jacket, which was slumped over the back of a chair near the bar. His shirt, replete with frills down the middle, was pulled taut across his gut, and he was still sweating profusely. Charlie drank eagerly from the pint Thomas set before him on the counter. Jean Evans, who unusually had stayed on with Charlie, and Mary Smith asked for gin and tonics following the lead given by Pat. Frank Harris and Alf Smith had pints, and David pulled two halves for himself and his father. An awkward silence prevailed for a while and then Thomas rang up the order on the till and, taking a handful of change from his trouser pocket, he put in the right money.

There was much chat about the old songs being the best, a conversation in which David took no part lest he be teased by his father or mother that no one could possibly understand what the words were in these new pop songs, which amounted to nothing more than loud guitars and banging on drums. Charlie Hawkins went on to argue that these pop groups only mimed anyway, and how there was an art to using a hand microphone. David took no part in this stage of the evening's proceedings either, for he had no wish to tell the chairman that his songs were frequently off-key and pathetically over-elaborated. He contented himself by thinking how better it would be for all concerned if Charlie simply choked on the mike one evening.

Occasionally, Thomas or David would refresh someone's glass and some money from Frank and Alf to pay for the drinks put in an unexpected appearance, though none as yet had emerged from the recess where Charlie kept his. David was surprised when he looked at the electric clock behind the bar - the plastic one with the cavorting figure of a deer and the logo 'Babycham' written all over its face - to find that it was gone midnight. Suddenly there was a loud banging on the front door, which halted the conversation immediately - it had moved on to Charlie holding forth about how difficult it was to reproduce the nuances in some of Sinatra's songs, and to David thinking that he'd have settled for the chairman getting either the words or the tune right.

At the door, opened by Thomas, were two policemen. The older one strode past Thomas and walked straight into the club and gave everyone there the once over; his eyes, just visible underneath his low-slung helmet, darted from one person to the other. The fresh-faced officer followed Thomas back to the bar where Thomas stopped and looked directly at the first policeman.

-How you going on then Tom? asked the officer.

-Can't complain Pete, said Thomas to the sergeant. What you having then?

-Oh! That's very good of you Tom. I'll have a pint, he replied with a beaming smile now directed at all and sundry.

Thomas turned towards the other officer who looked unsure.

-Probationer, said sergeant Hopkins crisply by way of explanation to Thomas.

-Oh, I see. What do you want to drink son? Thomas asked in a slow deliberate rhythm.

-Thank you very much Mister Rhys, he began.

-Tom or Thomas, interrupted Mr. Rhys.

-Thank you very much...Tom, he went on again as Thomas and the sergeant exchanged a glance. Can I have a half of mild please?

The sergeant seemed momentarily displeased.

-Half of mild? he queried with scarcely veiled sarcasm.

Thomas served them both and then introduced his son to the sergeant.

-You don't know my boy David, do you Pete, he stated.

-No. Pleased to meet you, said the sergeant as they shook hands across the counter.

-Where do you work? he asked.

-The lad's helping me out at the moment till he can get another job, cut in Thomas before David could say anything.

-Well, you could do worse than working with your dad, son. He's a good 'un. Anyway, I hope you get fixed up soon. Ever thought about joining us? he said finally with a smile.

-No, don't fancy it, replied David.

The sergeant looked at his colleague, two years younger than David, who was standing awkwardly on the edge of the group sipping his mild self-consciously.

-I don't blame you either son, said the sergeant. So, what's new then roundabouts? he continued. I was out puppy walking with the sprog, saw a light on inside, and thought it was time young PC. 258 Allen Marsh yere should learn a thing or two about how to work his patch.

-And what are you teaching him tonight then? asked Alf Smith.

-How to get a free pint out of old Tom there, chortled the sergeant heartily.

-You'll have to bring the lad back Pete, said Thomas in a gently chiding tone. He's only managed a half this time around.

Everyone laughed at the joke, and since the young probationer sensed it was not meant harshly, he joined in himself, and immediately he felt much less ill at ease. He even drained his glass with gusto.

-Another? asked Thomas of the uniformed lad, and everyone was looking at the PC closely.

-No. I'll have a pint of bitter, if I may, he said solemnly, and everyone laughed once more.

Thomas pulled him his pint, and another for the sergeant, and everyone else had the same round as before, and Thomas paid, but only for the drinks for himself and the others, not the two pints for the policemen. There followed some speculative talk about who might be responsible for a number of break-ins at small shops in the area, during which Plod's name was mentioned as a likely candidate by Frank Harris and enthusiastically supported by Mary Smith. The police sergeant shot David a look when he heard Plod's name, but there was no reaction on his face and David added nothing to the speculation.

-Well, we'd better be off, said the sergeant presently.

-No time for another? enquired Thomas.

-No thanks Tom. Mustn't have the sprog yere learning too fast now. See you again. Goodnight all.

David unlocked the front door and let the two officers out. When he returned to the bar Charlie Hawkins was remonstrating with Alf Smith.

-It don't matter Mr. Secretary, he said pompously. They shouldn't oughta have their drinks for nothing.

Charlie put on his jacket, as if ready to leave, but did not attempt to replace his bow tie. He turned towards Thomas.

-I don't approve of you giving 'em free drinks, he said sucking in his stomach slightly.

-Why ever not? asked Pat spontaneously. Christ knows you get enough cowing free ones.

-You'll not address me like that woman, said Charlie sucking in his gut all the more. I'll have you know...

-There's only one thing you need to know, Thomas interrupted. You'd better go now while you can.

There was an immediate stillness in the room except for Thomas who quietly and simply began to collect the beer mats on the counter and put them away. It was if he was saying to Charlie: 'I'm perfectly calm and I'm going about my normal business, but if you're not gone in a minute, it'll be the last time for a while that you ever open your mouth again like that to my wife'. And although it was unspoken Charlie heard the message, and his retreat - despite the hatred that boiled within him - was made easier by Frank Harris telling everyone that it was late and time to be off before the evening was spoiled by words said in the heat of the moment.

Making forced conversation and being overly jovial, Frank and Alf gathered up Charlie and, with the two women in tow, they left the club by the back exit. David went after them to bolt the alleyway door. All the shutters had been pulled down when he returned to the bar, but there was a fresh half of beer waiting on the counter for him, and he watched his mother who seemed to be trembling as she poured some more tonic into her gin. Thomas was sitting for the first time since stop tap, but David could see that his father was recovering from a sharp bout of coughing that had happened while he had been outside to lock up.

-I'm sorry Tom. I should have kept my big mouth shut, said Pat with a deal of irritation.

-You're not going to have an argument are you? asked David looking from one parent to the other.

-No, said Thomas after a pause. There's nothing to argue about. Charlie Hawkins was in the wrong and that's an end to it.

He leant forward in his chair and rested his arms on his knees and watched the smoke from his cigarette spiral up in front of his weary face. Pat moved towards him and caressed his back softly with the palm of her hand.

-Tom, I've never liked Hawkins and I know I shouldn't say anything to him to get him going, but I hates the way he's always taking advantage and coming on all indignant. He's such a cowing hypocritical windbag, but I am sorry if I've caused any trouble.

-Don't you worry yourself now, there's a good girl. I'll not let anyone speak to you like Hawkins was about to do.

Thomas looked up at his wife's still pretty face and he felt both happy and sad. Happy that he had lived his life with her and had known so much passion when they were younger; and happy too to have a son like David who was standing nearby. He knew that David wanted to protect them both. But he was sad that he should have brought them both to this. It was not for himself that he minded, though God knows it was becoming harder and harder to keep ahead of the struggle. There seemed nowhere else to go now at his age, and there were all the things he wanted his wife and son to have, but there seemed so little time left.

-Do you remember the night at the Pally dance in Tredegar, he asked Pat, when that lad came over and asked you to dance while I was at the bar getting drinks?

-The one with the funny parting in his hair, said Pat.

-That's the one. And you shouldn't have said anything about it really but you did anyway.

-I told him he looked like someone had parted his hair with a meat cleaver.

-He didn't take too kindly to that, did he?

-I hadn't wanted to dance with him anyway but you were a devil of a long time at the bar. I wanted to get rid of him some way, said Pat.

-Oh, you were managing that all right, said Thomas with a smile. But before he left he was calling you a few choice things when I returned to the table. No matter what you'd said there was no call for him to mouth off like that.

-The next thing I knew, you gave him a bunch of fives and he was sat on his backside with a quizzical look on his face, said Pat.

-And he still had that funny parting, added Tom. So, I couldn't have hit him all that hard.

The retelling of the tale drew them spiritually closer. David moved next to his mother and put his arm around her shoulders.

-I'd have done the same tonight if Hawkins hadn't shut up, said Thomas.

The three of them were joined one to the other now: David embracing his mother, Pat stroking her husband's back, and Tom still sitting but having reached out to hold his son's arm. Within the small circle was an unassuming love. The smoke from Thomas's cigarette still rose up in twisting columns between them, and then Thomas was shaken by a bout of coughing and the protective spell was broken.

At the bottom of the road Alf Smith and his wife said goodnight. Frank Harris accompanied Charlie and Jean into Ribley Street where he too took his leave, adding that Charlie shouldn't fret over a measly couple of pints. As they entered the house it wasn't the thought of the free pints that burnt so painfully within Charlie Hawkins, it was the sense that he had misread the situation and been completely outmanoeuvred by the steward, and in front of others too to make matters worse. Jean was about to go up to bed when Charlie saw several envelopes lying on the hall floor.

-Don't you ever clean this place up? he shouted at Jean who was at the foot of the stairs.

Charlie violently kicked the front door shut and then grabbed Jean by the arm.

-Answer me! he bellowed at her after he had spun her round. Do you have to leave it like a pigsty?

-They must 'ave come second post Charlie, she pleaded pitifully. I've been out all day or I'd 'ave put them on the mantelpiece for you.

But Jean knew as the sickening in her stomach grew worse that there was no rational excuse that Charlie would accept, who now held her roughly and pressed his face up against hers so that she could smell the beer on his breath and feel the heat of the sweat breaking out on his forehead.

-It fucking looks like you've been out all day, he screamed at the frightened and cowering animal before him caught in his trap.

With all the pain and humiliation welling within him he suddenly struck Jean high up on the right side of her face with a sharp backward stab of his forearm. Jean fell away from him but not completely to the floor for he still held her with his left hand around her wrist. She struggled to be free so that she could scramble away or at the least sink to the floor so that she could roll up into a ball and try to hide from the blows. But he held her with naked malice, and called her a no-good dirty slut and a lazy bitch, and all the time as he towered above her, deaf to her screams, he hit her without pause across her head and shoulders until his fist was bruised by the sheer weight of blows. When Jean was unconscious Charlie finally let her fall to the floor where he left her as he retired to bed.

CHAPTER SEVEN

Peety Malone's mother had wrapped him up well against the dank November air that seemed to penetrate to the very bones and settle upon them with a calculating chill. He hadn't liked the way that a big nasty-looking man had greeted him when he had stopped at the house to drop off the groceries. And the lady the big man had called to the door appeared to Peety to be so ill; it was not a nice thing to be poorly, he told himself. Peety had even asked his mam about the lady's illness. She had said not to worry for the lady had fallen down the stairs a few weeks ago and she would be better again soon. So Peety, whose heart was naturally touched by any suffering he encountered, asked his mam if the nasty-looking man were looking after the ill lady, because if not he didn't mind running more errands until she got better. His mam answered that Charlie was doing his best to look after the lady, and it was wise for Peety not to get too closely involved in other people's business. She could see that her son was still puzzled, if no longer concerned, and to take his mind off it she told him to pop along to Mr. Morgan's to find out if he needed anything from the shop. When Peety got there he knocked on the door for some while but received no answer. He decided to go and find Mr. Morgan in order to help him with his shopping, since Peety supposed that was where he'd gone already.

The game was going badly for the side in red who were already twenty points adrift and taking a fearsome mauling from a much heavier pack of opposing forwards whose still white jerseys testified to their ability to keep their feet and drive on mercilessly. Old Man Morgan was very glad that the two teams had jerseys of such distinct contrast for he found it almost impossible to tell the difference at times, especially if both sides became all muddy. In fact, his senses were now so dulled that he hardly noticed the stench from the glue works settling over Smelly Park. He had set off from home with the vague memory that there was usually a game in the park on Saturday afternoon. And there was another feeling too, which he had now forgotten, but which had something to do with going outside. It was an unpleasant feeling, he remembered, like fear. He had not been outside his house in... (he could not recall). It seemed very strange to be dressed for outdoors - he checked to make sure that he was no longer in his pyjamas and red dressing gown - but the walking stick felt familiar. So did the isolated seat in the middle of Smelly Park, and the rumbling noise in the distance (he supposed of traffic) had a reassuring ring to it too. He heard the shouts and cries of the players. They were getting closer he thought to himself.

As if emerging from a fog the teams came into Old Man Morgan's view. There was a line-out directly in front of the park bench. A faint whiff of liniment reached his nostrils, and he just heard someone shouting 'best effort now boys'. How he loved the game. It was many years since he'd played last but all the sights, sounds, and smells were still locked away in his mind. But there was something unfamiliar about the contest before him; something that was not quite right. He pulled out his watch fob and gazed at the inscription trying to remember what it was that was different. Slowly he realized that in his youth he had been a football player but the game he was watching now was different. It was rugby, a game he had never played, but the smell of embrocation, the manly voices urging on one's team mates, and the sounds of players grunting to reach the ball, to make the tackle, to do one's best - these were just the same as ever, as if he were on the field himself playing his beloved football.

Old Man Morgan wasn't sure what to do with this realization; he felt a certain anxiety but about what he did not know. His attention was brought back to the game by a loud blast of the referee's whistle, which seemed to cut right through the mist now falling over the park. 'Crooked throw' he heard the referee shout and then, 'Reds, do you want it taken again or a scrum?'

The two sets of forwards packed down five yards in from the touch-line and directly in front of Old Man Morgan who was trying to focus his eyes on the scrum. As the No. 9 fed the scrum, he could see the surge of the white pack trying to push their opponents off the ball, which the hooker had won for the reds on their own put-in. The white-jerseyed tight-head prop was trying to drop his shoulders below those of his loose-head adversary so that he could propel him upwards until he popped out of the scrum and would be useless to prevent the opposing pack from driving on and claiming the ball. The red prop with his legs like tree trunks was resisting this ploy with all his might. The pressure on his neck and shoulders was enormous and he prayed that the scrum half or the No.8 would pick up soon and bring an end to his torture. But although the veins on his neck looked fit to burst, his muscles ached with the effort, and the opposing prop was like an eel twisting and turning to drive him up, he was staying down; staying down to the end even in a lost cause.

In what seemed no more than a blinking of an eye to Old Man Morgan the ball was passed from the base of the scrum, the forwards broke off from their deadly embrace, and the game moved beyond the sole spectator's sight. He could no longer hear any voices nor the whistle, so he imagined the game must have ended. He had to return somewhere, (to home that was it), but the park was murky and the way was unclear. He shivered with cold, and became bewildered by the length of time it took him to get sufficient purchase on his stick to prize himself free of the seat. After a slow succession of halting, painful steps Old Man Morgan reached the fence surrounding the park. He touched the fence with a frail outstretched hand and thought immediately that he had become trapped inside a huge cage where unknown dangers lurked in the gloom, and he felt a rising panic. Blindly he staggered along the fence where fortune led him to the gate and the exit; but instead of turning towards home Old Man Morgan shuffled silently towards the Brownhills and gradually he faded from view in the mist and his own confusion.

The mist had first turned into a fine drizzle and then into persistent rain so that Peety Malone pulled up the collar of his baggy coat and peered into the shops. There had been no sign of Old Man Morgan in Joneses, nor in any of the shops on Coronation Road, so Peety had set off for the small arcade at the start of Dock Road, which was just beyond the boundaries of Riverside. But there had been no trace of the old man in the arcade, and now Peety was stood on the concrete concourse wondering what he ought to do next. He decided he would wait a while longer to see if Mr. Morgan would turn up.

The steady rain of the last hour was beginning to wash away the cigarette butts surrounding a still patient Peety. The shops had closed and Peety was alone on the concourse, but he had not noticed any of these things for, in his innocent desire to be faithful and to help others, he had become transfixed with only one thought and one mission, which was to share the burden of Mr. Morgan's shopping. It was a good thing he did now, he thought, and even if Peety had some hazy notion that his mother might be worried by his prolonged absence, he felt she would applaud the noble sentiments behind it; and so he waited afresh and lit another cigarette. His spiky hair was almost all now plastered to his skull by the rain. Occasional violent movements of his head, like a horse tossing its mane, sent the droplets spinning away from his head, but his coat - someone else's cast-off - hung lower and lower under the weight of water that was soaking into it. Hidden within an inside pocket were Peety's cigarettes and a box of matches. As he grew more anxious about whether to stay longer or to give up his honourable, but as yet futile cause, he slipped his fingers around the packet of Woodbines in order to feel something familiar and reassuring.

Into Peety's well-focused but limited world, in which he knew little of the rancour and chaos of what is called everyday life, there came a gang of four boys from the Pringle estate. They dropped their brash walk and their banter of braggarts as they entered the shopping concourse and approached warily the figure before them - the strange-looking dolt in the ridiculous coat who stood there jerking his head occasionally and smoking a fag nervously. It was the sound of their slow footfalls that first set off the pangs of anguish within Peety. When he looked up and saw the four youths spread out in an arc silently converging upon him, he felt that he was being hunted and he realized, too late, that his line of retreat had been cut off for behind him were only the locked and closed shops. The youths were no longer wary; rather they were fascinated by the creature they now recognized as the stupid cretin who lived in Riverside and who went about, so it was said, pretending to shoot people. None of them had met Peety in the flesh before and each was eager to find out what sort of show the crazy man would put on, so they came right up to Peety and stuck their faces into his and called him foul names.

Poor Peety did not understand that the gang was only looking for some fun. For the first time since a night many years ago when he had lain awake in bed thinking of what his life would be like without his mother, and the only answer to that thought had been his heart pounding remorselessly within him, he felt his heart now beating faster and faster and seemingly growing larger and larger so that he believed it must split open. It was fear that he recognized within himself, (not fun), the same fear he had known that night of an unimaginable world in which he was alone and where there was only darkness and the sound of a frantic heart. He knew that something unnatural was happening; that vile intruders were breaking into a world he had supposed was eternally safe and devoid of threat, and he gripped the packet of Woodbines so firmly that his fingers began to crush them.

One of the boys knocked the remains of Peety's cigarette from his lips with the tips of his outstretched fingers, and they all laughed when a look of astonishment mingled with fearful apprehension appeared on Peety's unshaven face. They pretended to hit him again, each one taking a swipe at Peety's forehead and then watching their victim duck and dive to avoid blows he had no way of telling were never intended to land. All the while Peety's right hand protected his precious Woodbines inside the deep pocket of his cavernous coat.

-C'mon you stupid sod! Let's see you dance or whatever it is you do, called one of the youths.

-Yeah, c'mon, parroted another.

-Don't just stand there you crazy bastard. Shoot me down! said the first with growing exasperation.

-Yeah. Shoot, shoot, shoot, they chorused together.

Peety dared not focus on their faces - the first glance had been enough for him - for it was as if he had glimpsed the torture of hell where flesh was despoiled by torment and suffering. To Peety these were evil and contorted faces, and he instinctively turned away from them. But to the four gang members it seemed that Peety was being furtive and was hiding something. He had been their quarry and they had enjoyed the manner in which they had toyed with their capture, even though they had been unable to make Peety draw his gun by virtue of their ignorance of the magic words. Their attention might soon have waned but for the idea, which now crept into their minds, that Peety might have on him something valuable, something they could wrestle from him and take away as a great prize to mark the encounter.

Now that they were no longer flicking out their hands at Peety's head, nor taunting him hysterically with awful names, it was not long before they noticed Peety's right hand clamped inside his coat.

-What'yer got there? demanded one of the youths on behalf of the gang.

Peety gripped more tightly and turned the right side of his body away from them. It was if he had given them a signal for instantly they fell upon Peety, who began to kick out at his assailants as they tried to force his hand from the coat pocket. One of his clumsy kicks caught one of the gang on the knee causing the youth to lash at Peety's head in retaliation. The ring on his finger cut into Peety's bulbous cheek and he cried out in terror as he felt the blood begin to flow. The others succeeded in removing Peety's hand from where they believed he held his treasure, largely by ripping the pocket itself from the coat, but still they could not unwrap Peety's fingers. Peety continued to howl at the top of his voice but his cries only urged them to more violence to finish the job. At last, they wrestled Peety to the ground and one of them stood on his wrist until slowly and painfully Peety unfurled his fingers to reveal the prize.

-Shitty Woodies! cried a youth. A packet of fucking fags, that's all.

-What a jerk, called another as he jeered at Peety who was still lying on the ground.

-We don't want these fuckers, said a third as if they had all been unfairly denied a well-deserved reward for their endeavours.

Peety reached up with his battered fingers.

-Peety's Woodbines, he implored.

The gang looked on impassively at Peety's entreaties. They were unmindful of the loss they had caused him and of the pain they had introduced into his world. Henceforth, Peety's path would be strewn with fissures and cracks and crevasses, so that he would always feel a dread of falling into darkness and of hearing his heart explode. He beseeched them again for his cigarettes, still unable to comprehend why they had been taken from him in the first place. He knew that his cigarettes had been stolen - his mam had told him that stealing was naughty and that God punished those who were naughty - but he was unprepared for the knowledge that God would punish him so painfully. Perhaps if he could get his cigarettes back, he could make amends for the theft, which somehow - he did not know how precisely - was his fault. And so, he begged them for the return of his Woodbines, but now the youths had turned sour. What had at first been an object of ridicule and an unwilling vehicle for their amusement had become a figure of scorn. They grew contemptuous of the oaf lolling in front of them begging for something that was already destroyed. One of the gang took the tattered and torn cigarette butts and rubbed them into Peety's lips and tried to stuff them into his mouth. Peety stopped calling for his Woodbines but his eyes overflowed with tears, and the pounding in his heart settled into a steady and dreadful rhythm.

Mrs. Malone had spoken to her neighbours some hours earlier and a number of them had put on their coats, picked up their umbrellas, and gone off in search of Peety, for it was most unusual for him to be missing in this way for so long. The word had reached some of the children too who joined in the hunt with gusto and treated it like the game they supposed it was. Even Plod, who was anxious to show that he was still a leader, got involved. First, he dispatched a group of lads to scour the riverside from the boundary with the Brownhills upto the abandoned sand yards. Then, he collected Cavie and set off purposefully to inspect the surrounding streets. It was luck, (not God), and the fact that they had already covered most of the streets in Riverside that brought Plod and Cavie to the shopping concourse just as Peety was being assaulted.

The two of them took in instantly what was going on and without any hesitation Plod exploded into action, running at the group of youths and throwing himself bodily into them with a vengeful determination. Two of the gang immediately scattered, and Peety simply covered his head with his hands and cried in anguish while still lying on the wet concrete. As the three fighters disentangled themselves from a heap, Plod turned immediately on the one whom he had seen rubbing something into Peety's face. Instinctively, Plod decided to stuff something appropriate into his opponent's own face, which he achieved with a head butt across the bridge of the youth's nose. The lad crashed to the floor stricken and his nose spread in a bloody mess across his face. Plod was about to put the boot into him when the other youth caught him with a kick to the side of his ribcage that tore the breath from his body and made Plod stagger under the blow. He turned towards his assailant and managed to parry the punches with his forearms but only at the cost of being thrown off balance. Immediately, the youth saw his chance and was about to kick Plod between the legs when Cavie brought him heavily to the ground with a flying tackle. They grappled together on the floor where neither one could land a telling blow until Plod, now almost fully recovered, grabbed the youth around the neck and hauled him up thus allowing Cavie to land several punches to his defenceless midriff. Cavie stopped his assault when he heard the boy beg for mercy, whereupon Plod released his hold and the boy sagged to the ground and cried in pain.

Plod and Cavie left the two gang members where they had fallen and walked the few paces to Peety who, still on the floor and acting in an agitated and distressed manner, was trying to pull his coat over his head. Plod knelt down next to Peety and took hold of the lapels of Peety's coat and gently pulled them down so that his head was entirely visible. Cavie tried to dab away the blood on Peety's face but he was startled by the stinging touch of the handkerchief on his cheek and recoiled immediately. Each of them told Peety that everything was okay; no one was going to hurt him anymore; they had sorted out the gang; and they would take him home. Slowly, Peety calmed down and they managed to get him to stand up but the sight of his erstwhile attackers caused him to shrink away and to become ever more agitated again. Cavie approached the two youths who were still gathering their senses and trying to handle the pain and humiliation and told them to be off instantly or they'd get more of the same. The two picked themselves up and limped back to the Pringle estate. Plod watched them go thinking to himself that he'd put one over on the estate gang. He was pleased with his performance and no matter how Cavie embellished his own contribution, he would at the very least be able to confirm the story that Plod would recount to the Riverside lads that he had beaten off four opponents and rescued Peety.

As Peety was escorted back into familiar territory he became appreciably quieter and his whimpering had almost ceased. Plod got out a packet of cigarettes and offered one to Cavie. Peety watched the cigarettes being lit and there was a new intensity etched into his face. This time he took the offered handkerchief from Cavie and slowly he rubbed at the dried blood on the side of his cheek.

-Peety's Woodbines, he sobbed at last.

His plea never wavered and for the rest of the journey home he looked at Plod imploringly and asked for Peety's Woodbines. When Plod could stand no longer to hear the anguish in Peety's voice, he gave him his packet of cigarettes, which Peety examined carefully. Then, very deliberately, he took out each of the cigarettes in turn and as best he could with his trembling fingers he snapped off the filter tip and returned it to the packet. When he had done this for the whole pack, he selected one and lit up, drawing on the smoke at length and hoping that it would transport him back to his safe world. Plod and Cavie felt a kind of relief when soon after they knocked on Peety's door and left him with his mother.

Betty Sawyer wished earnestly she was not so fat and unmanoeuvrable for she was distressingly out of breath and she was sure that red hot pokers were assaulting the soles of her feet, so painful were they to her. She had not been at all reluctant when she heard the news to go out in search of Peety - his poor mother had looked so worried - but she was now just about at the end of her tether and despite her umbrella she was wet through. There was no sign of Peety at all in Smelly Park and Betty was standing by the exit and steeling herself to carry on her search further along Coronation Road when two children ran towards her. They were still too far away for her to hear what they were shouting, but even when the children halted by her side she could barely make out their garbled message. Eventually, as they tugged frantically at her coat and told her to hurry up, she learnt that a man had been found lying unconscious in the Brownhills.

Although Betty felt that her chest must surely explode and her feet were unable to take her a step further, the incessant urging of the children drove her on across the slippery mounds and past the water-filled hollows until, at last, she saw a crumpled figure on the gravel with another child on both knees beside it. She staggered towards them entirely breathless and was unable to say anything for some while, but she saw immediately that the figure was Old Man Morgan who was being comforted by the eldest of the three children who had found him.

-We were out looking for Peety Malone, explained the eldest girl. We found Mr. Morgan right yere, and I thought he was dead at first and we were all frightened and about to run away, but then he started moaning so I sent the two nippers to get some help.

-You did very well, said Betty after a while, doing her best to reassure them all.

She bent over to look at the prostrate form. Rivers of rainwater were running down his face, which even in the gathering darkness appeared grey and flaccid, and his breathing was shallow and ragged.

-You two off home now, she said to the two children who had first found her. There's nothing to worry about.

She watched them scamper off and she could see that they were glad to be away.

-You must go straight to the 'phone box by the post office on Coronation Road and ring for an ambulance, said Betty to the remaining girl. You dial 999. Have you got that? Tell them to send the ambulance to the Brownhills, and when you've done that wait by the park to show them the way.

The girl nodded to show she knew what to do and then ran off as fast as she could. Betty cradled Old Man Morgan's head in her arms and tried to keep the rain off him with her umbrella.

-It won't be long now, she told him repeatedly.

The hospital said Old Man Morgan was suffering from exposure, but it was really old age. And since he was old and they needed the beds for other cases the hospital sent him back home a few days later. Betty Sawyer and a few other women in Granall Street kept an eye on him and brought him his meals until the social services caught up with his needs. It was an effort to get him to eat anything so steeped in dreams and lethargy had he become. Two weeks later one of Old Man Morgan's sons turned up on the door and after a short visit promptly went away again. A few days after that both sons were seen at the house talking to the social worker and making other arrangements. One Friday an ambulance pulled up and a stretcher was carried in. Old Man Morgan emerged into Granall Street for the last time securely strapped into the stretcher. A small crowd had gathered around the ambulance where David, who like the others had gone along to see what was happening, caught a brief view of the old man's face as they carried him to the vehicle. His eyes were clear but full of sadness, and he lifted his hand feebly as if to halt the process of his betrayal. For a moment Old Man Morgan's hand remained raised, the uncut and twisted nails reflecting a pale, yellow light, and then it fell back to his side. His flesh was already becoming pinched and drained as if the blood in his thin veins could hardly be bothered any more to circulate fully throughout his body

-Mother! Mother! he cried out as his gaze swept back towards the house where he had lived an entire lifetime.

David heard one of the sons say to the other that the old boy must really be out of it for his mother had died ages ago. Fancy calling for her now thought some people in the crowd, and they put it down to the fact that he must be terribly upset as well as confused. But David remembered the day he had returned to Old Man Morgan's to rewire his fire when he'd told him that mother was the term he'd used to refer to his wife ever since the time the two boys had left home. As Old Man Morgan tried to lift his head in one last attempt to drink in all around him that had meant so much - had been his entire life - his two sons had already gone back inside the house and were busy dividing between them the bits and pieces worth keeping. The ambulance doors slammed shut and Old Man Morgan was taken to a home where there were lots of others like him. He was not there many days before he died. His sons seemed hardly able to stick around for their father's funeral before they were off back up north again.

Peety Malone seemed much the same on the outside when his mother told him about the death of Mr. Morgan. He knew that dead people were taken away in big black cars and he did not appear to be upset by the thought. He had even resumed gunning down challengers after a short period in which he had spurned all advances to do so, much to the incredulity of the children in the street. He still ran errands, but now there were times when he wondered what might be around the corner, and every time he saw a big black car he asked himself whether he might be responsible for Mr. Morgan's death because he had not helped him with his shopping. The innocence had gone out of his life.

CHAPTER EIGHT

The yard at the back of the Rhys's home was a bit of a tip. There was no grass nor earth only concrete and brick. When he lived in Tredegar, Thomas had the mountain at his back door and after returning home from the pit and washing from a zinc tub, he had often walked on the hills behind his home. It was called a mountain but it was nowhere near as big and grand as that. The sheep, which were such a nuisance when they got into the back gardens and ate the flowers and vegetables, roamed at will across its slopes. On the hills closest to the floor of the valley a few sets of pens and an occasional hut used by the pigmen broke up the mountain's rounded slopes, but for the most part the hills were bleak and prone to partnership with seeping mists. Not much grew there save for the rough grass clipped by the sheep. There had been a time a generation and more ago when the hills witnessed a different kind of growth - the kind that stirs in men's hearts when a vision of a better world is put before them. Thomas Rhys had often gone to the gatherings on the hillsides and listened to the oratory of Nye Bevan whose words filled men living in desperate times with hope. During these meetings it had sometimes felt to Thomas as if he were hanging on the words of a preacher promising not spiritual salvation but social justice. Thomas had long ago ceased his own religious devotions but he well remembered how his mother gently chided him every Sunday as she got ready to go to the Presbyterian Chapel while Thomas determinedly read the paper, or rushed off to help one of his brothers repair a bicycle - anything, in fact, but accompany his gentle mother to hear more empty words.

And where were they now? One brother was already dead, the others had moved to England in search of work, and his mother and father had long since passed away. Men no longer gathered in hushed expectancy on the hillsides and Nye's dream of social justice had not been fulfilled. As far as Thomas was concerned the Labour Government straight after the war had made many changes for the better; the life people had now was virtually unrecognizable from that in the thirties. But the squalor and the decay were still there - they had only changed colour. He was right, Thomas often told himself, to have left Tredegar when he could no longer work underground for there was no future there. But he still missed the small back garden. Like many men who work deep under the ground he took immense pride in using the earth to grow strong, healthy plants. Even the marauding sheep could not blunt the fine harvest of leeks nor dull the glorious colours of the flowers he used to grow. But here in the yard between his house and the club there was no fine crop, save that of bottle cases, and no rich earth, only an uneven and flaking concrete floor.

Thomas Rhys was not the sort of man who would be easily defeated, however. Around the walls of the yard were a dozen pint bottles, formerly full of beer and now topped up with soil, which were hanging by the neck from pieces of string attached to nails driven into the brickwork. Growing out of their bases, where Thomas had punched holes with a metal spile, was an array of geraniums whose stems wound upwards around the brown bottles before the plants exploded into snatches of colour. But everywhere else inside the yard was a mess, not so much because there were large quantities of abandoned materials - in fact there were virtually none - but because the whole place was so untidy and dilapidated.

Bottles of beer, flagons of lemonade, and siphons of soda water all came in varying sizes and in different boxes so that it was impossible to arrange all of the empties in the yard in a well-ordered manner. The best that could be done was to stack Mackie cases together, lemonade cases together, and so on, until a crazy matrix of columns of boxes of different heights and sizes had been built between the lock-up bottle shed and the Rhys's back door. Opposite the door to the bottle shed, whose corrugated asbestos roof was filled with green moss and black muck, were the coke and coal bunkers. Built side by side the coke bunker was the larger of the two, but each suffered from dilapidated brickwork and ancient wooden flaps that let through the rain and threatened to collapse finally into pieces every time they were opened to allow fresh deliveries to be thrown in. Next to the bunkers were three extremely old and battered rubbish bins; there were only two lids. It was through this untidy hemmed-in enclosure whose physical fabric was slowly unravelling that Thomas passed each time he went to work in the club. Even the approach of Christmas made no difference, for the patterning of bottles and cases and the decay of the bricks and wood went on just the same.

In the club itself, however, the onset of Christmas did mean changes. No one in Riverside was rich and few were what could be described as comfortably off. Christmas, therefore, put a strain on family budgets, especially for couples with children, and particularly now so many people in the area had been thrown out of work. While people could not afford to be profligate with their cash, they were equally determined to have a good time at Christmas, (if you can't enjoy yourself then what's the point?), and to ensure that the children had decent presents, (well, it's all about the kiddies at Christmas, isn't it?). Most of the members of the Coronation Road Working Men's Club joined the 'Xmas Club' and saved small sums with it each week throughout the year. The club treasurer, Tony Newbold, would count the money a member handed over and enter the amount in the person's savings' book, and a week or so before Christmas Day everyone would come into the club and draw out what he or she had put away to pay for the children's toys.

Christmas time also produced the happy coincidence of being able to enjoy yourself, as you would normally, and to stand a chance of picking up some much-needed extra cash. So it was that from the start of December onwards the club members played bingo with a special urgency in the hope of scooping the prize; they selected their weekly tote numbers with extra care and with added oaths to bring them luck in the draw; they bought tickets to the Christmas raffle in the fond belief that they would win chickens and hams and tins of biscuits in the lottery; and they played the one armed bandit with increased gusto positively willing it to drop the jackpot and to ease their financial burdens.

Then there were the decorations. Each year they were brought down in their boxes from the committee room upstairs and the permitted few - usually wives of the committee men - would ceremoniously unpack them. Often the trimmings needed to be repaired with cellotape and sticking plaster before they could be re-used - the committee rarely sanctioned the buying of new Christmas decorations in the belief that there was nothing wrong with the existing ones. After the essential repairs had been made, the bunting and rolls of brightly coloured paper would be strung around the club. Large shiny red and blue and green spheres would be unfurled and the dust blown away from the paper leaves before they were stuck, in strategic positions, to the yellowed and peeling ceiling. Frank Harris or Steve Curtice, who each owned a battered van, and a small number of committee man would collect a saw and make the short journey to the Forestry Commission's land just outside Cwmporth and would return with a fine Christmas tree. Back at the club the illicit tree would be decked in spluttering lights and deluged with crinkly swathes of multi-coloured tinsel. Thereafter the tree would proceed gently but persistently to drop its needles in front of the portrait of the Queen as if seeking revenge for the indignity heaped upon it.

Sprigs of mistletoe were hung up about the club and above the bar shutters where Pat Rhys eyed them darkly, for she couldn't conceive of wanting to kiss any of the club members never mind the cowing titty men. At least Pat had control over the decorations inside the bar itself. Each year she put up fresh holly, and in between the bottles of spirits on the shelves she placed little models of Santa Claus and his reindeers, and on the hand pumps she tied compact Christmassy bows in bright colours. But the bright colours did not reflect her own state of mind about the festive season. For one thing, the Christmas period was damned hard work for Pat and her husband, especially as there were late night extensions on Christmas Eve, Boxing Day and New Year's Eve. While some clubs remained closed on Christmas Day until the evening to allow their stewards and stewardesses to enjoy their own family dinners, the Coronation Road club actually opened rather earlier than normal in the morning to allow members to pick up their raffle prizes. There were always more people in the club over the holiday than at other times so the pace behind the bar never let up, especially as hardened bitter drinkers would suddenly decide at Christmas to have a tot of rum or whisky to go with their regular tipple.

But it wasn't just the work; it was the clear impression conveyed to Pat and Thomas that their Christmas, their family celebrations, were to be secondary to the institutional needs of the club and the personal enjoyment of its individual members. It was not malice so much as bloody-mindedness that brought about this state of affairs. 'We pays them to work so that we can all have a bit of a laugh and a good few drinks over the Christmas' was how chairman Hawkins had put it at a recent committee meeting where Thomas had requested half-day closing on Christmas Day. While a good time would be had by all prior to returning home to have their Christmas dinners, Pat would have both to work behind the bar and try to cook her own family's meal.

She achieved this by doing all the preparations for the meal early in the morning. She would put the turkey on a low gas just before she went to help her husband in the club and thereafter took whatever opportunities she could to leave the bar, run down to the house, and check the meat. When David had been a boy, Pat's quick sorties into the scullery would be accompanied by encouraging words to her son, who usually became hungrier and hungrier as the afternoon wore on, that it wouldn't be long before the bar shut and they could all eat together. But when that time came Thomas was tired and simply wanted to relax before the evening's onslaught of renewed heavy drinking by the members, while Pat was anxious to give David his meal as quickly as possible, yet fretted that the meat might not be properly done and the gravy too lumpy. The upshot was a meal consumed in haste, a few crackers were pulled and everyone wished one another a Happy Christmas, and then Thomas would fall asleep in the chair as David manoeuvred his toys around his outstretched feet, and Pat - feeling the loss of a time that should have been special like any normal family Christmas - did the washing up in the bosh.

Her resentment was almost tangible but as a child David had never recognized it, caught up as he was with his new guns and toys and games. Later, when David did realize his mother's feelings about Christmas, he was unsure what to do. He had suggested to her that she shouldn't worry so; that it wasn't all that important, but this had only made the abnormality of arrangements for Christmas dinner more keenly felt by Pat. Then David had mentioned, in passing, that perhaps he could help with the cooking, which made Pat feel even worse. She hated cooking but she recognized all too easily when her son was trying to be nice to her because he knew she was upset; and the fact that it was clear that David knew about her feelings caused her to plumb new depths of resentment against the committee. While Thomas was essentially a stoic when it came to Christmas, (he could take it or leave it), Pat was at heart a traditionalist, and the denial of a traditional family Christmas was to her another indicator of all she fought so hard to keep at bay, which was nothing less than the dissolution of her marriage and the break-up of her family. She did not fear these things because of a falling out of love, or of taking one another too much for granted, but because of the drudgery of surviving.

It was early December, the miners throughout the country were operating an overtime ban; the Government was shiting itself and introducing measures to curb the levels of street lighting and to reduce temperatures in offices; there was talk of a three-day week, but the normal bingo sessions at the Coronation Road Working Men's Club were in full swing as if nothing were amiss. Indeed, for many members it was absolutely necessary to put such things behind them when entering the club; it was alright to argue the merits or otherwise of the miners' case, but it was seriously frowned upon - on club premises - to get depressed about what a forthcoming coal strike might mean for your own job.

Charlie Hawkins was in unusually good form. He had always prided himself, and bored others, with the belief that he was a most efficient bingo caller and tonight he felt that his voice had never sounded clearer. His big, normally clumsy hands had become transformed into deft manipulators of the numbered chips that he pulled, one by one, from the large velvet bag and carefully set down in their allotted places on the housy board. Each chip was selected at random but the hands moved with metronomic precision so that the time between calling each number was the same, and every game of bingo thus moved to a reassuring rhythm. The players knew exactly how long they had to scan their cards to see if they had the number called; even people like Mary O'Flaherty and Betty Sawyer who often marked four or five cards per game had sufficient time to check all before them.

With the approach of Christmas, most people bought extra cards to mark since this increased their chances of winning a line or a full house. The faces of the bingo players were not stern, rather they were serious as if everyone in the room was studying for an important examination. The caller looked serious too for he had to make sure he spoke clearly; there would be hell to pay if someone missed a winning number because it had been called indistinctly. But as far as Charlie Hawkins was concerned looking serious meant appearing important, and so he relished bingo nights and his role within them.

-All the fours, forty-four, called Charlie in his steady manner. Two and eight, twenty-eight. Lucky for some, number seven. On its own, number five. Kelly's eye, number one.

Between each call the silence seemed to grow even deeper as every person in the room listened in tense anticipation to hear if someone else would claim the game. Cigarettes smouldered untouched in ashtrays or on the edge of tables until a call of 'house' cracked the audience's silence and unleashed a logjam of chatter and eager comparisons of bingo cards as the winning numbers were checked. Then cigarettes would be reclaimed, or new ones lit, and glasses would be raised to thirsty lips, fresh rounds would be purchased at the bar, gossipy conversations would pick up again where they had halted, until Charlie would shout 'Best of order ladies and gentlemen. Eyes down now for the next house', and the steady, hypnotic game of chance would begin all over.

Since Charlie was the permanent centre of attention while the games were on - winners lived in the limelight only briefly and were sometimes the subject of disparaging remarks suggesting they were too bloody lucky by half for people who didn't come in the club all that often - it was not incumbent on him to go to the bar to slake his thirst. Someone else brought him his beer - the doorman, another committee man, or whomever he nodded to to show that he was ready for another. Nor was it seemly that the great caller should pay for his own beer; in recognition of the valuable service he was performing for the club and its members, he awarded himself four cheques for his evening's work. One of these small tokens he would give to the man who was fetching his beer so that it could be exchanged at the bar for a pint. Cheques of this kind were also awarded by Charlie to himself and to others for putting on a good turn at the concert nights.

Much to Charlie's quiet annoyance the crowd did not settle down until the second request for good order and, as the members now stared intently at their cards with their pens poised expectantly, Charlie deliberately delayed the start of the new game for some seconds. A few heads looked up and when Charlie felt he had made his point and reasserted his authority, he called eyes down and selected the first number. Just to the side of Charlie, the gaudy Christmas tree still rejoiced in its vengeful mood and had dropped copious pine needles, which scrunched underfoot whenever anyone went past. Above the chairman's head a long roll of Christmas decorations sagged despondently from the ceiling; it would have to be rehung in the morning. These things, however, did not matter to the players. The only thing that could disturb their concentration would be the sound of the one-armed bandit, so during bingo sessions the machine was turned to face the wall like some impudent and noisy child in need of disciplining.

Mary O'Flaherty had not even won a line at bingo never mind a house. As soon as the last game ended - with a win for that peroxide blonde marking only one card, the lucky cow! - Mary dashed to the bandit at the back of the club. Even as one of the committee men was still in the process of turning the machine around, Mary had stuffed a coin in the slot, grabbed the handle, and thus claimed ownership.

-Ooh, pardon me for getting in your way, said a disappointed punter to Mary who ignored the other woman's sardonic smile.

-You can carry me winnings back to the bar for counting if you like, said Mary sarcastically to the woman who returned to her seat and pointedly indicated to her husband that the bandit would probably now be occupied all night by Mary O'Flaherty.

Time spent playing the bandit was indeed a sore point among many of the members. Although there were no rules about how long a person could play the slot machine, those who hogged the bandit aroused considerable resentment, especially when the club was busy. With Mary there were only three ways someone else could get to play the bandit if she was in possession. First, she might run out of money, but provided she had had some modest winnings during the course of her play, this could take some while. Second, if you were a friend of hers and stuck around long enough by the bandit and congratulated her on her skill at coaxing down the yellow bell or the bar sign and commiserated with her bad luck when the reels cruelly overran, Mary might invite you to go halves with her. But this option applied to relatively few club members since Mary did not bestow her friendship lightly. Third, someone might approach Dec, Mary's husband, and suggest that perhaps Mary was feeding the machine just a little too much of the housekeeping money. But this seldom worked because Dec liked the quiet life and was somewhat afraid of his wife when she was in full spate on the bandit; she never looked that way when he was having her in bed and the intensity of her commitment to gambling coin after coin he found oddly threatening. You might think there was a fourth alternative; that dropping the jackpot would mean Mary's gracious withdrawal to count her winnings. In fact, she never left the machine after having won the big prize without feeding it some more money just in case it was going to drop again.

Charlie Hawkins cleared away his numbered chips and board and took them back upstairs to the committee room. A group of people entered the club through the front door letting in blasts of cold air, which gave the tree yet another excuse to shed its needles. Thomas Rhys put his hand on the large, ungainly radiator behind the bar. It was lukewarm; the stove needed more coke putting on. David and Pat were busy serving thirsty customers and there was no sign of the doorman, so Thomas decided to go and fetch some coke himself.

Outside in the yard the sky was clear and full of stars, and a frost was already creeping across the wooden flap of the coke bunker and settling on the empty bottles in their cases. Thomas lifted the flap and picked up the shovel, which lay on top of the mounds of coke, and quickly filled a bucket with the grey lumps. The dust from the coke began to irritate his lungs, but he did not stop to cough; instead, he went quickly into the club, opened the door of the stove, and threw in the fuel right to the back of the chamber. He did this three times in rapid succession and as he emerged again into the yard to fetch one last bucket of coke, he was conscious of having worked up a sweat. He would have returned inside straightaway to avoid the sweat drying on his skin in the cold air, but the growing constriction in his chest prevented him from doing anything other than trying to catch his breath.

Thomas stood by the bunker and wiped his brow. A familiar pounding in his head was beginning as he tried to clear the obstruction with a series of short, sharp coughs. The veins on his neck throbbed under pressure as the degenerative process gathered pace. His tall body was now bent over - Thomas's arms were braced against the wall of the bunker as his torso was rocked back and forth by the powerful eruptions. His attempts to draw in sufficient air were mocked by the sound of a rasping wheeze. Within his red and puffy face, Thomas's eyes had become watery and blood-shot, and spittle dripped from lips that trembled under the effort to clear a path for the air. His lungs were now raw, and the pounding at his temples made Thomas feel he wanted to scream, but there was no breath to do so. Just when he felt that he could no longer withstand the jarring of the coughing, somewhere inside him it was as if a bubble had burst freeing the constriction, and he was able to draw in gulps of air, which slowly eased the pounding and reduced the unnerving throb of blood through his tortured veins.

Sent by his mother to find out what had delayed Thomas, David became immediately alarmed when he saw his father who was still bent over and whose chest was heaving up and down to the accompaniment of scratchy, distressed breathing. He was covered in sweat and was beginning to shiver violently. David took one look at his father's distraught figure and urged him to go inside the house. Slowly Thomas raised his head and, with some difficulty, drew in a long breath of air.

-I'll be fine, he wheezed. Leave me be for a few moments, there's a good lad.

-You should go to bed dad and lie down, said David trying not to sound as if he were admonishing his father.

Thomas indicated with a feeble wave of his hand that he had not the breath to reply, but he took David's proffered handkerchief and wiped the beads of sweat from his face, which was pale and unrecognizable as the warm, friendly face David knew.

-Take your time now dad, said David not knowing what other advice to give.

He thought of running back to the club to tell his mother, but he quickly dismissed the idea for he knew that such a course would only embarrass his father and needlessly, perhaps, upset his mother. He'd had such attacks before, though David had to admit none had ever seemed as bad as this. His father was apparently incapable of moving from the bunker, which had become the only thing holding him up, but as yet no one had come out into the yard and seen him in such a state.

Under the cold stars, father and son stood silently together against an uncaring world. In the background could be heard the sounds of a hundred voices all merged into a single low murmur as the life of the club stirred afresh. The noise of the ratchet on the bandit's one arm carried above the rumble of conversation, as did the clatter of coins into the winnings tray. Thomas's uneven breathing gradually became steadier but took on the timbre of a rattle and inside his lungs a million needles pierced every piece of their fabric and filled his being with a pain he had never before experienced. Very slowly, he unbent his body and released his hold on the bunker-wall. Thomas looked all about him, then up at the stars, and finally towards David.

-Better get back to work, said Thomas in a way that left no room to doubt, or to resist, his determination to return to the bar.

There was nothing more to be said between them. No further words could make any clearer the understanding they had, nor alter the moment before them. Thomas moved along the yard towards the club resolutely if somewhat unsteadily at first, while David watched him on his way. In that moment David tried to imagine what courage it could be that got his father out of bed each morning racked as he was so often by scything fits of coughing. Any man might be discouraged by the sheer physical effort he went through sometimes simply to release the suffocating tautness within his chest and to draw breath. But courage was not enough, it occurred to David. Pride was not enough either; it was love of wife and son that drove Thomas Rhys on and that made him in David's now tearful eyes a man who walked head and shoulders above all other men.

At the door of the club Thomas hardly hesitated at all, but opened the door just in time to hear Mary O'Flaherty curse her luck on the bandit. Charlie Hawkins stood at the foot of the stairs but remained unacknowledged by Thomas. After David had wiped away his tears and inhaled deeply to compose himself, he too returned to the bar. For the rest of the evening David was gripped by the fear that his father would suffer another collapse, and he watched him closely even at the cost of inattentiveness to the orders he was given by the customers. Thomas himself appeared to be in a daze, working on automatic, but somehow he finished the night. Although David said nothing to his mother about the incident in the yard with his father, Pat Rhys knew that all was not well and that into their lives something fearful and repellent had entered, which even now was creeping around her family and sniffing about for signs of weakness.

CHAPTER NINE

Elaine stood on the riverbank and stared across the swirling expanse of the Effyl, which was flowing silently towards the sea. She was thinking of Stomper and worrying that she had been partly responsible for his death. The wind caught her hair lying softly along her back and blew it across her pretty face, wiping the tears from her cheeks as the fine strands were swept back again. Through her tears she imagined the body of a young man floating away on the tide before her. She could not help remembering, although she felt uneasy, even unworthy with the thought, that Stomper had a fine body. It had briefly excited in her feelings of sexual desire that had been far removed from those she experienced with Cavie. Over the summer when Stomper had worn what amounted to a casual uniform of blue jeans and an assortment of T-shirts, Elaine had discerned underneath his clothes a lean body with quick purposeful movements. To her, Stomper had been care-free and vibrant where Cavie was moody and intense. She remembered how Stomper was always combing his fine hair in an affected manner, but his vanity seemed to sit easily with his confident approach to life. Stomper had been someone who could explain things in a light, convincing manner and who could talk about events and turn them to his own advantage. Cavie, however, usually said very little, but Elaine could sometimes guess what was going on inside him by the watchful way he always looked at her as if he were stalking an animal and waiting for a sign to attack.

She had been surprised the afternoon of the bonfire to run into Stomper at the top of Ribley Street and to find him so agitated. Elaine's surprise turned to concern when she heard Stomper's account of his fight with Cavie and, when she realized that the two had been fighting over her, she was at once fearful and elated. Her fear sprang partly from uncertainty about what Stomper knew of her liaison with Cavie, but mostly from disturbing thoughts about what Cavie might do next. She had always suspected that simmering beneath Cavie's rough exterior was a well of violence waiting to be released. Elaine felt too that Cavie wanted increasingly to possess her, not just sexually, but more deeply and in such a way that he could signal to the world that she was his property. She feared this fight with Stomper might cause Cavie to look for a way to brand her with the mark of his ownership. Even as Elaine decided it would be better to avoid Cavie if she could in the future, her heart leapt at the sight and sound of Stomper stood before her recounting his victory.

Stomper had painted Cavie as an unrelenting opponent who in the end he had lured onto the horns of defeat not by greater strength but by superior wit, and Elaine had listened spellbound. Then he had asked Elaine what she saw in Cavie and Elaine had blushed deeply, shamefully, and had been unable to give Stomper an answer. But Stomper had not demanded an answer - his victory, she sensed, was complete without the need to dominate or humiliate her - instead he had suggested to Elaine that she could do better for herself than Cavie. Elaine had looked away, but Stomper gently had cupped her face in his hands and tilted her head upwards towards his gaze. He had simply smiled at her and then told her she was the most beautiful girl in Riverside. No one had ever looked at or spoken to Elaine like that before. She found herself agreeing joyfully to Stomper's request to take her to the bonfire, despite her anxiety that such a course would inevitably lead to seeing Cavie again so soon after the fight.

Without anything having been said explicitly between them they had both recognized that a pact had been made; Elaine was henceforth going out with Stomper as his girlfriend. After Stomper had left, telling her he would call back later that evening, Elaine had begun to wonder what Stomper would want of her. As yet, he had not even kissed her - an intriguing fact that impressed Elaine deeply - but she knew that she would have to decide soon how far to let him go. His hands on her face had felt soft and warm, even caring, and she had tingled with pleasure at the thought of them exploring other parts of her body and of his lips pressing against hers in long, passionate kisses broken only by the sound of his breathless voice whispering how lovely she was. And if Elaine then said no, not all the way, she believed Stomper would pull back; she felt she would not have to do the things she and Cavie had done because she knew the alternative was worse or because she sensed she had no choice. Whatever she and Stomper might do, and Elaine had not been sure if she would allow him to go all the way, she was certain that Stomper would respect her.

And now he was dead. All she had ever done had been to press her lips against his thigh when he had emerged triumphant from the river, like an unredeemed promise of pleasures to come. But she had seen the hate-filled look on Cavie's face and she knew that it was her presence by the fire that had driven Stomper to ever greater demonstrations of bravado at Cavie's expense. The guilt cut deeply into her even as the Rush's undertow had dragged poor Stomper to his doom, for to Elaine it was clear that she had played her part, albeit unwittingly at the time, in delivering Stomper to such a fate.

The wind grew stronger and whipped Elaine's long hair into a frenzy of chaotic activity. Patterns of ripples appeared on the surface of the Effyl. There was something distasteful about the river. It was not the mud and the grey water; rather it was the sense of the Effyl being a conduit along the edge of Riverside into which all the effluence of the town might be discharged. The sewerage outfall a short way upstream from Elaine had its course marked by slime-covered stones that stood out like chancres against the dark mud. Strewn along the rocks of the sewer were pink prophylactics, crumpled and exhausted, and thin straggly lines of spent toilet paper. Occasionally a gull would screech down to pluck up a morsel and then would fly off quickly before others tried to deprive it of its catch. On and on the sewage cascaded down the rocks and into the Effyl and with not so much as a by-your-leave to the people who thought of the river and its banks as a part of their own community.

Elaine wanted to be rid of the river, its smells, and the encompassing mud, which seemed capable of sucking you under and destroying you. She wanted to be somewhere other than Riverside whose decay and drabness were reflected in the greyness of the Effyl. It was no more than the idealized romantic dream of an adolescent, but in Stomper - for the briefest of moments - Elaine thought she had glimpsed a better future, not one that would have necessarily taken her away from Granall Street, but one where there would have been some decency and love. Most of all Elaine dreaded a future like her mother's where men, thick with the smell of beer on their breath, groped you with nicotine-stained fingers and then abandoned you when they had finished their snatched pleasures. Only slightly less dreadful, because of the mixture of mind-numbing boredom and thankless activity it entailed, was an early marriage and soon a life full of snotty kids and an inattentive husband. Such a fate had less excitement to commend it than even the incessant tides of the river, which made the Effyl rise and fall with predictable regularity.

Elaine could no longer stand motionless, shivering against the cutting wind, so she began to walk along the embankment towards the Brownhills. She would almost have been out of sight from the landing stage, had she not paused at a bend in the river and allowed her thoughts to dwell once more upon her loss, when Plod and Cavie appeared on the dirt track close to the suspension bridge. Plod had been invited, in the disingenuous words of the letter from the dole office, to attend for interview to discuss his job prospects. But Plod, in his quiet way, knew well enough that the interview wasn't going to be about finding him a job so much as a confrontation in which it would be decided whether to suspend his dole. Cavie was supposed to be accompanying Plod to the dole office, not to provide moral support but to tell lies on his friend's behalf; namely, that the two of them had practically worn out the soles of their shoes tramping around Cwmporth in a fruitless search for work.

-Look mate, I don't think this idea of yours is going to work, said Cavie who had been less than convinced in the first place by Plod's plan.

-I'd do the same for you mun, replied Plod rather petulantly.

-Yes, I know that, but you've no hopes of fooling 'em with this. You'll drop a bollock if you drag me into it. They'll want places of firms we've supposed to have visited, dates we were supposed to be there. It'll all get too frantic, said Cavie.

-How do you know all this then? asked Plod.

-Same thing happened to my brother and it got 'im nowhere fast too. You've got to talk tidy like to the people in the dole office. Make 'em think you're okay.

Plod began to give some thought to this advice, which at first he was unable to consider on its merits because it came from Cavie, who was normally so dumb. While Plod mulled it over and considered an alternative approach to the forthcoming interview, Cavie caught sight of a figure disappearing towards the Brownhills. He recognized instantly that it was Elaine and that here was an opportunity to speak to her alone. He turned back towards Plod impatiently and hoped that he would not be detained much longer in convincing Plod to give up his stupid idea.

-Talk tidy, is it? said Plod eventually.

-Yeah. Hold the stuff about looking for work back, and only give it to 'em if they asks you, urged Cavie.

-And what it they do?

-Well, you can give 'em a few details, but not so much they can check up on you. It's your attitude to work that counts; they ain't looking to find out if you was outside Woolies at nine o'clock last Saturday asking for a job as a storeman. It's what happened to my brother. Gospel!

-Righto, said Plod. I'll go on my own, and I'll see you later.

-Count on it, said Cavie who was relieved to see Plod set off towards his appointment.

Cavie turned around to look at the riverbank leading to the Brownhills; it was deserted now but Cavie was sure he could still catch Elaine before she made it back to the streets.

As Plod entered the Labour Exchange he bumped into a man who was hurriedly leaving the building. He seemed eager to be elsewhere, but his shabby overcoat ingrained with dirt and his unwashed and smelly body clearly indicated he had nowhere decent to go to.

-Sorry cap'n, he said to Plod in a voice that struggled to retain mastery over the baleful influence of the bottle of cheap sherry he had already consumed.

-Leg it! ordered Plod who was in no mood to strike any charitable pose to someone he considered to be a scumbag.

The drunk staggered across to the toilets and disappeared down the steps with many a lurch and stumble. Plod thought it an absolute disgrace that they gave money to such down and outs, but he consoled himself with the thought that maybe the coppers would arrest him and lock him up. Little did Plod suspect that with the weather turning so cold the scumbag in question would soon be actively pursuing such an option, since a warm police cell was better any day than a freezing park bench. Anyway, continued Plod's vein of bitter thought, there's not much good the coppers can do with his sort. They pick them up now and again and remove a few from the streets, like they do with the kids into theft and joy-riding cars, but they're soon back out. The coppers are just like seagulls swooping over the sewers; no matter what they pick up, there's lots more on the way. If you want to sort out these alchies, there's only one way to do it, and that's to stop giving them any money. It's not like they want to work, so they shouldn't get anything; that would gee them up.

Plod's own current lack of work he viewed differently from that of the drunks and the bums. These people were just taking advantage and would never change if you kept on giving them the wherewithal to buy more drink. But Plod would willingly take a job, if there were any decent jobs around. Plod did not see himself as workshy, nor as someone on the scrounge; rather he was someone who resisted for as long as he could the intention of the dole office people to palm him off with the shitiest jobs they could find. He knew he had a poor education, no qualifications, and no skills - unless you included breaking and entering - but Plod was damned if he was going to let anyone exploit him by stuffing him into a dead-end job with poor wages to match, and where you were expected to give all but could expect fuck all in return.

The face behind the hole in the wall told Plod he was late for his appointment with Mr. Watkins and that he was to wait, appropriately enough, in the waiting room until he was called. Plod sat down at the back of the room that was painted in an awful coffee-coloured gloss, which had once gloried in the name 'Burnt Brazil'. The high walls hung menacingly over the claimants who came here, as if threatening to fall on those who were intent on making false supplications. Officials, almost as pissed off as the unemployed and the down-on-their-luck to whom they supposedly provided a service, lurked unenthusiastically behind glass panels, protected from whatever contagion these citizens brought with them to the office. The impression was distinctly one of trying to block the undeserving so that the state might be saved the bother of determining their rights. Plod patiently awaited the start of the process to sort the chaff from the wheat.

The uneven texture of the seat was uncomfortable and Plod moved further along the bench only to reveal a deep carving in the wooden surface, which said 'Sod off'. He was chuckling quietly to himself when he became conscious of someone looking at him; it was a disapproving look.

-Leonard Probert? enquired the official.

Although Plod looked up, he did not answer for Leonard Probert - his actual name - was something he had not responded to since he'd left school.

-Leonard Probert. You're late, stated Mr. Watkins.

-So I've been told, answered Plod and he stood up to face the man who had already decided this was a piece of chaff before him, one of the undeserving.

Plod was briskly ushered into a drab office and with a perfunctory wave of the hand he was invited to sit on a metal-framed chair with a shiny plastic seat. On the desk in front of him was a sign saying 'Mr. G. Watkins: Employment Officer'. The other objects on the desk-top looked as if they had been placed meticulously, and in the centre lay a buff-coloured folder bearing Plod's proper name in the top right-hand corner. A business-like Mr. Watkins sat down opposite Plod and opened the file, studying it closely for some minutes in silence.

-Well, Mr. Probert I see we haven't been gainfully employed for ten months and two weeks, said Mr. Watkins as he looked over the top of the file, which he now held before him like a barrier to keep the contagion at bay.

-I have been out of work for about that time, confirmed Plod who stressed the personal pronoun in the hope of conveying to Mr. Watkins that he didn't like his patronizing tone.

-Quite so Mr. Probert, said the official with a faintly derogatory emphasis on the mister as if he could barely bring himself to apply the common courtesies.

-And during that time you have signed each week confirming that you were available for work and that you had undertaken no paid employment? Is that correct Mr. Probert?

-Yeah, that's right. I sign every Thursday morning.

-Not quite every Thursday, I think. You signed a day late recently I understand.

-Yeah, I was, as you say, helping the police with their enquiries that particular morning, said Plod with a smile.

Plod's last comments were ignored by Mr. Watkins who placed the file flat on his desk and removed a letter from it. He spent some moments re-reading the ill-formed, almost childish, handwriting scrawled across the single page of the letter.

-So, he said with a hint of accusation in his voice, you have never taken any paid employment during the period under review.

The official began to sort out internal memoranda, which were used to record telephone messages, and placed all four of them one under the other on the right-hand side of the file. Plod could not read what was written in the letter or in the memoranda but he had been through this before in different circumstances. Despite the close eye contact from Mr. Watkins, Plod's thoughts drifted off towards the criminal court where a figure in a funny black gown read from the same official-looking pieces of paper; they were the charges or accusations about what you had supposedly done. And another even funnier-looking geezer in an off-white wig with a plum in his ever-so-high-and-mighty mouth said daft things like 'I put it to you Mr. Probert that on the night in question you did willingly receive the said goods knowing them to have been stolen. Is that not so?' What sort of a way to talk was that for Christ's sake! This Mr. G. Watkins: Employment Officer wasn't as clever as the posh guys in wigs and gowns, but he did the same job, thought Plod. One way or another, whether it was the police, the lawyers and judges, or the petty Hitlers at the dole office - they all tried to fuck the poor.

-Mr. Probert! You received no payment of any kind? insisted the man behind the desk.

-No money at all, said Plod with what he hoped was an air of finality.

-Then how do you account for these reports (he swept his hand across the pieces of paper laying on the file) that you have very recently been seen engaged in manual labour for which it is alleged you received payment? Payment you did not declare, added Mr. Watkins for good measure.

-How can I account for things I know nothing about? answered Plod calmly.

-So, you deny that you know anything about November 29th 1973 when at 38 Ribley Street you were observed demolishing an outhouse in the rear garden? You deny too, no doubt, that on the 1st December 1973, again at 38 Ribley Street, you effected repairs to the plumbing system and upon leaving the dwelling you were offered and accepted a sum of money from the occupier, a Miss Joan Napier.

-Thirty-eight's where my sister-in-law lives, said Plod hardly believing what he was hearing. Joan's married to my brother and she needed someone to pull down a small outhouse; it was unsafe what with her toddler crawling around the back.

-And the plumbing? asked Mr. Watkins.

-Hardly plumbing mate. She had a dripping tap and I brought round a few tools and fixed it for her.

-And the money?

Plod blushed suddenly, which seemed to confirm Mr. Watkins's suspicions. It was amazing how they crumbled when faced with the evidence, he thought, and he allowed himself a satisfied grin.

-The money? he pressed.

-Joan asked me to go to the chemists to buy some (Plod paused) some, er, nappies cause the kid had the squits and she'd run out of stuff to change him with.

Now it was Mr. Watkins turn to disbelieve what he was being told, and the sense of being deprived of what had seemed an assured and quick victory made him alter his tactics.

-Joan, you say. Miss Joan Napier, in fact. In further fact, she is not married to your brother at all, is she Mr. Probert?

-Not legal like, but I always think of her as Billy's missus. She's family.

-Hm. But in point of fact no matter what you think about Miss Napier she is not family, she is not a relative, she is not legally your brother's wife.

Plod was wondering how such a pillock could be so spectacularly stuck-up when he was thrown off-balance by the next question.

-If what you say is true, that you were merely helping a, ahem, friend of your brother, why could not your brother do these things himself?

Mr. Watkins sat regarding Plod with an even more satisfied smirk growing across his face. Plod shifted uneasily in his seat and seemed confused as to what this had to do with the reason for the interview.

-He's away, Plod said at length.

-Is not Mr. William Probert a guest of Her Majesty? suggested Mr. Watkins with barely suppressed enjoyment.

-There's no fucking need for that, responded Plod immediately. Yeah, Billy's in the nick. What's that to do with you?

-Claimants do not speak to me in that tone of voice, began Mr. Watkins

-What tone of voice do you want me to tell you to fuck off in? interrupted Plod.

Mr. Watkins's previous calm air of innate superiority was now under severe threat. He sensed a greater hostility in the young man opposite than was normal at these kinds of interviews, and he became alarmed to notice Plod fingering the tattoo on the side of his neck. He considered the possibility that he may have gone just a touch too far in bringing up the topic of the brother's incarceration; it wouldn't be long, he felt, before this one too was locked up in prison. Anyway, he had heard sufficient - the excuses were ridiculous and there was more than enough still on file, which he had not yet raised with the claimant, to justify his actions. Mr. Watkins took a form from the file, filled in some details, and then turning to look again at Plod he closed the folder.

-I am less than satisfied by your explanation. Your weekly payment of unemployment benefit will be suspended forthwith pending a full enquiry. You will be informed of the process and your rights in this matter in due course. Good day Mr. Probert, you may leave.

Plod got up immediately and left the building. A passing policeman was ignoring the drunk whom Plod had bumped into earlier. At least you know where you stand with the coppers, thought Plod. These other characters in the dole office want to screw you for acting normal and trying to be human. He was still thinking about the injustice in the world as he made his way back to Riverside.

Cavie found Elaine by the long grass and the tall reeds where the two of them had met before. His sudden arrival had caused Elaine to spin around swiftly and Cavie noted that the startled expression on her face immediately turned to one of trepidation when she had recognized him. However, Elaine did not run away for she realized that Cavie would easily be able to catch her; instead, she tried to swallow her fear and to stand as casually as she could contrive while Cavie approached.

-Hiya, said Cavie in a bright manner that came as a surprise to Elaine who was expecting something more threatening and sullen.

She nodded a silent response to Cavie's greeting but could not bring herself to look at him full in the eyes.

-I miss 'im too you know, continued Cavie, again to Elaine's surprise.

-Who d'you mean? Stomper? she asked petulantly.

-Who else? Cavie replied. I suppose you misses him the most of all.

-Why d'you say that? said Elaine warily.

-You was soft on 'im, wasn't you? It looked like it at the bonfire.

-That was ages ago and Stomper is..., she hesitated.

-Dead, said Cavie with a chilling finality. But you was still soft on 'im all the same.

-What if I was? said Elaine turning slightly away from Cavie to look out over the river once more.

-I thought we was going out together like, he said.

Cavie's voice sounded harder now and when Elaine eventually steeled herself to catch a glimpse of his eyes, they were dark and brooding. She turned her back on him even more.

-I bet you never turned your arse on Stomper, spat Cavie suddenly.

-What's that supposed to mean? she shouted, and because she was angry she turned around to look him straight in the face.

-Don't play the innocent with me; it won't wash. I bet he was all over you and you loved every bit of it. I bet you was even doing it behind my back before the night of the bonfire, wasn't you, you little cow?

Cavie's squat body stood before her barring escape and the intensity of his gaze grew fiercer so that Elaine began to shake with fear. He saw her shaking. Through her unbuttoned coat he caught sight of her small breasts and the erect nipples trembling under the thin material of her blouse, and lust pumped through Cavie's veins. He made a sudden lunge towards her and caught her by the shoulders. His thick lips pressed down onto her face with enormous force, searching to join with her mouth, and then his right hand roughly inserted itself under her coat and began painfully to squeeze her breast. Elaine tried to twist away from his ugly embrace.

-No you don't, shouted Cavie and he pulled her back towards him and jammed her hips between his legs and rubbed his swelling cock along her body.

-Leave off, screamed Elaine.

-I bet ol' Stomper didn't leave you alone did he? Kept you well serviced. Eh? Eh?

-Shut your filthy mouth! We didn't do anything!

-Oh, said Cavie coyly as he released his grip on her slightly. Why bother to take up with 'im then if you weren't doing anything?

Elaine's head dropped and some of the spirit seemed to depart her body. For a while she remained silent, conscious of Cavie's laboured breathing and his hard cock digging into her side. She felt degraded and imprisoned.

-Because he was kind to me, said Elaine at last in a whisper.

-Wanted to get inside your knickers is more like it, sneered Cavie who buried his hand inside her coat once more and held her to him as he frantically sought her lips.

-You like that don't you, you little bitch? said Cavie and when she didn't answer he shouted again, don't you?

She could feel him pressing more urgently against her, his lust growing harder and harder, and she knew that she must give him what he wanted. She prayed he would settle for that, as he had always done before when, in order to deflect his ultimate desire, she had told him he was too big to go in her, she was underage, and she had no protection. Then before he could counter her arguments, with force she feared, she would take his longing for her and render it spent. It was this she did now. Elaine sank to her knees and even as she unzipped Cavie's greasy jeans his cock fell out into her face. Quickly she took hold of it with her practised fingers and drew his foreskin back and forth, back and forth, waiting to hear his moans and to confirm that one imperfect manner of escape was in hand. But Cavie's hands gripped Elaine tightly on either side of her head and he guided her mouth towards his cock.

-Suck me! he screamed. Suck me!

Like an obedient but fearful child, who wishes to avoid further punishment, Elaine did as she was told. She curled back her lips, as if in a snarl, and allowed the tip of his cock to enter her mouth. She felt it brush against her teeth and heard Cavie gasp and tell her to be fucking careful. Then she felt Cavie insistently pressing forward while holding her head steady and she allowed more of his length to slip inside. Cavie pulled back with his hips and then thrust forwards again; in and out, in and out, slid his cock, and Elaine's lips enclosed its girth and caressed it, and Cavie moaned with an animal-like quality she had never heard before. After what seemed a lifetime of being gripped by fear and loathing and lust, she felt Cavie explode and she tasted the semen as it slid down her throat.

Cavie stood over her with a triumphant grin on his satisfied face. He ignored her coughing and gagging and put his cock away as if it were a trophy going back inside its case. As Elaine got up from the embankment she noticed the familiar muddy patches on her knees. Cavie offered to take her home but she said there was no need, and he left her with the reminder that he would see her again. Elaine's heart sank at the thought and she wondered how she had ever started up with Cavie. She should never have believed him when he begged her to wank him to relieve the awful pain in his balls, but she had been curious and had wanted to taste the power of it all, to control a brute of a body like his, to hear him moan to the rhythm she played on his cock, and to bask in his breathless thankyous when she had finished him off. She should have stopped, she told herself, when Cavie started to want to have her all the way, but she felt she could still be in control. Now it was his power she had tasted; his mark had been put inside her; and she no longer felt worthy of any vision of a life beyond Riverside.

CHAPTER TEN

Normally Thomas Rhys would have gone to the bank himself. Every Thursday morning he counted up the week's takings as soon as he got behind the bar so that he could pay them in just after the bank opened. With less than a week to go before Christmas, Thomas had placed a large order with the brewery. All the clubs and pubs in the town were laying in extra and with so many barrels and cases to supply the dray had not been able to deliver at its usual early morning time. Indeed, it had still not arrived when the Coronation Road Working Men's Club had opened. Fortunately for Thomas, Tony Newbold had dropped into the club to get something from the committee room (he had explained), and the treasurer had offered to bank the takings himself so that Thomas wouldn't miss the dray delivery.

When the dray eventually arrived and the barrels had all been lowered one-by-one onto the shelves in the cellar, the lorry drove around to Granall Street so that the beer cases could be carried in through the yard to the bottle shed. The dray men were a good bunch and, while David started to sort out the barrels, and his mother served behind the bar, they willingly helped Thomas to stack the cases in the shed. Finally, the dray men carried the cardboard cases full of spirits to the bar where Pat put them away out of sight in the cwtsh under the stairs.

-Thanks lads for giving a hand, said Thomas to the dray men.

-Think nothing of it, Tom. Mind you, it's thirsty work now so it is, said the driver with a broad grin.

-Usual? asked Thomas. Or would you prefer something a little stronger seeing as it's nearly Christmas?

-Just a pint of shandy please Tom. Still got a few more deliveries to make yet. But it'll be the usual pints of bitter for these two labourers, I imagine.

His fellow dray men smiled at their mate's jokey description of them and then nodded their agreement and watched in anticipation as Thomas pulled their pints.

-Always a good pint yere, said the one as he drained most of the glass with a single swallow.

Thomas Rhys was pleased that his beer was appreciated and he rested his hand on the pump and smiled quietly to those around him as they sank their beers, licked their lips, and finally wiped their mouths with the back of their sturdy arms to remove the froth. Further pints were offered willingly but reluctantly only halves were taken up for the dray boys could not remain much longer if they were to get their work done.

-Just supervising the cellar work now is it, Tom? asked the driver who nodded in the direction of the open flap door and the sounds of barrels being shifted.

-Aye, that's the boy doing all the work down there, said Thomas.

-Building 'im up is you Tom for something special? suggested the driver's mate.

-No, the lad's helping me out; that's all.

-Good thing too Tom, said the driver again. You're looking a little off colour mun. Sure you're okay?

Pat looked up from the customer she was serving and observed her husband closely.

-To tell you the truth Bert, I haven't been feeling quite right lately.

-Chest again is it? asked Bert who was familiar with dust on the lungs since he was a valley man born and bred himself.

-No, that's just the same.

The look on Pat's face would have told a different story.

-I can't say rightly what it is but I feel dizzy like now an' then, continued Thomas.

-Well, take it easy then, said the remaining dray man.

-Chance would be a fine thing with Christmas coming up, said Pat with a smile, but with a slight edge to her voice.

It was high time for the dray men to move on and goodbyes and Merry Christmases were exchanged, and the driver assured Thomas that if needs be they could fit in another delivery on Christmas Eve, and they all told him to take care and hoped he'd be feeling better soon. The three of them left telling one another that you really did get the best pint of bitter in the town from ol' Tom and what a pity it was that he had such an awful cellar and had to work in a club full of so many shits.

Pat gave the change back to the chap who had insisted on just a dash of lemonade in his pint and then had moaned that there wasn't enough.

-Still feeling a bit off then? she enquired of Thomas.

-Yes. And my ankles are a bit puffy and swollen, he added.

-Not painful though? asked Pat, touching her husband's arm.

-No, no. Nothing like that. It's just a queer feeling I get from time to time.

-Why don't you go down to the house and have a breather for the rest of the afternoon. David and I can handle things yere.

Pat had not expected to win the day quite so easily, and she was genuinely surprised when Thomas had consented to her idea. Normally it was the devil's own job to get him to take time off when he was ill.

-It's not too busy, said Thomas as if by way of justification for his choice.

-That's it luv; we can manage. Go an' have a lie down or put your feet up and have a cup of tea, suggested Pat.

-Let me check with David first that everything's alright in the cellar, said Thomas.

Thomas descended the steep steps into the cellar and found David lifting some of the barrels of mild across to the next shelf.

-That's the ticket son. Now don't forget to put a few kegs of lager in by yere, said Thomas indicating the spot on the shelf with his outstretched hand.

-Righto dad, said David who had not forgotten his father's earlier instructions but was nevertheless pleased to hear these brief words of praise.

-Your mam's packing me off to the house to get some rest, said Thomas in his friendly way. You can take care of things yere, can't you son?

-You okay dad? said David who had stopped his work and was approaching his father.

In the poorly lit cellar, it was difficult to recognize the pallor of Thomas's face, especially as his head was bent over away from the fall of the light. Now that it was winter, the walls were covered with the stains of water seepage and of dark splotches of slime slowly sliding down the sides, and from the roof of the cellar hung grey droplets like engorged nipples spread on the underside of some grotesque bitch. Even bent over awkwardly as he was to avoid hitting his head on the roof, Thomas's hair brushed the droplets so that they fell from the ceiling and began to run down the side of his face.

-Bloody place, said Thomas as he wiped away the water and the tiny pieces of grit that had been suspended in the droplets. It's worse than the grave down yere.

-You go back up dad. I'll see to things. You get some rest if you're not feeling well.

-Oh, I'll be all right. Just need a little breather, that's all, said Thomas in as light a tone as he could manage.

-Righto. See you later, is it?

-And don't forget to shut the cellar doors at the front or you'll have the kids messing with them before too long, added Thomas as he climbed the stairs upto the bar.

-Anyway, David shouted after him playfully, what do you know about the grave? You always said to chuck your body on the rubbish heap when you went.

-Best place too, said Thomas to his son as he disappeared from view.

A shaft of light coming through the doors at the front of the cellar pierced the gloom surrounding David who continued to heave barrels into their allotted places. When he had finished this work, he made sure that all the pipes were free and unobstructed and then he tapped and spiled a fresh barrel of bitter, which his father had told him would be needed later that day. There were two enamel buckets full of beer to be filtered back into barrels and David set up the holder with its thick white filter paper and poured in the first bucket. The beer swirled around the sides of the filter holder and the paper ruffled softly as it wrinkled under the weight of liquid. David repeated the procedure for the second bucket and then watched with a quiet satisfaction as the beer slowly disappeared until only frothy rings remained on the filter.

As David began to tidy up, removing and disposing of the old filter papers and generally cleaning the passageway and shelves of spent corks, the sense of oppression he always associated with the cellar whenever he'd seen his father trapped within it, seemed now to be descending upon him, like a cold dead hand. David stopped his labours and stood silently, simply gazing along the narrow confines of the underground trench. His father had spent what amounted to a lifetime down here, he thought. And for what? There were no medallions for excellence in his work; there was no promotion to something better; there wasn't even a good pay packet at the end of each week; there was only this dank imprisonment. And upstairs above the cellar existed loud-mouthed boozers and a feckless committee. However did his father put up with it, David asked himself.

As he sought for an answer, David realized that he too was becoming increasingly enmeshed in the club and the demands of its members. No matter how many times he told himself that the work he was doing now was only temporary - he'd get another job as soon as employment in the town picked up - he was conscious of being under a kind of emotional restraint. Indeed, it was as if he were a captive, not only of the cellar but also of his father's increasingly poor health. It was that, more than anything else, which held him here now. Although David was not resentful towards his father, the feeling of being a captive of events beyond his control was not what he had intended when he had set himself to help his parents with the burden they carried. He didn't mind the sheer physical effort, much of which he took off his father's shoulders, nor the nights he gave up to serve behind the bar. He wasn't even worried by the chance of being shopped to the dole-snoopers, but David found himself wishing fervently that his father would get better - that he would be able to cope again as he had done all his life before. He wanted this not just for his father's sake but also for his own. In the past few months David had come to recognize that running a club was not a long-term job for him. You could not have a proper life, especially a family life, running a club. The hours were too anti-social. But it was more than that; it was having too many fools puffed-up with their own self-importance telling you what to do all the time because they believed they knew how to run a club better than the steward. It was about the endless inane chatter - sometimes spiced with spite - and the petty rivalries that always take hold in small cloistered communities. But, most of all, the thought of the gossip-laden relationships between the members, the mechanical sinking of pint after pint, and the bleak futility of the activities carried on within the smoke-filled, bingo-calling clubroom so depressed David that he could hardly bare to contemplate the possibility of being sucked permanently into such an existence.

The shaft of light at the far end of the cellar shimmered and momentarily disappeared as some children leaned over the flap doors to peer into the cellar. One of them cupped his hands to his mouth and shrieked out his name. The sudden noise made David jump and tore him away from his despondency. The other boys and girls followed their leader's example and they all began to call their names or to shout 'bugger' or 'bloody' and to listen for the echoes. In the confines of the cellar the children's screams seemed to scrape the crumbling brick from the walls and to jangle David's senses. David moved swiftly towards the flickering shaft of light beneath which the elongated shadows of the children's heads and shoulders played grotesquely across the metal kegs and the wooden barrels.

-Clear off you noisy young sods! he shouted as he remembered what his father had told him earlier about shutting the cellar doors.

The sudden appearance of an adult had made the children run away from the hole. But they had not gone far and David could hear them still, as he reached up to close and bolt the flaps, when at first they giggled at the delightful recognition of a swear word worse than they had dared to use, and then when one of them cried 'sod off yourself mister!' David paused in the act of lowering the last flap and stuck his head up so that it seemed to emerge straight from the pavement. He stared severely at the children - he was enjoying the role of angered adult immensely and was wondering if they would react as he had done as a child to interfering grown-ups. Warily, the group of boys and girls backed off a few more paces in silence. They were waiting for David's move. This was afterall their strip and they saw no reason to move away from where they had chosen to entertain themselves unless driven off by weight of superior arms. David admired their firmness but he was not surprised when, very suddenly, he threw back the flap so that it clattered to the pavement with a loud bang, started to climb out of the cellar, and saw the children run away with intermingled skips and shouts of 'sod off', 'bugger, bugger', 'bloody bugger'. David smiled broadly and watched them go; not for them yet the weight of an unrelenting and unrewarding existence.

A few minutes after running away from David, the boys and girls arrived flushed and happy at the top of Granall Street, where they renewed their games free, they hoped, from grouchy buggers who popped up from the ground to spoil their legitimate fun. Granall Street was a lengthy palindrome - the same tiny terraces with bulging walls and brittle bricks and rotten window frames, no matter from which direction you approached it. But the children did not seem to notice or to mind over much. They took it all for granted, for they were used to the squalor and had little conception of anything better. In fact, very little seemed to upset the children as they roamed their mucky playground like the tough little denizens they characteristically were, unless it be rancorous arguments between parents, which occasionally spilled out into the street itself and which would later result in a child being taunted by his fellows about his parents' slanging match - a fate often worse for the child than hearing the original argument. One popular version of the public bust-up was the husband returning late - too late and too drunk - from the club or pub. He might get to his front door to find it locked and bolted or even to confront his irate wife barring the way and spoiling for a fight, which would not only wake up the children in the house but half the street too. The man would insist on his right to enter his own home. Not in that state would come the reply. In any state he damned-well wished the woman would be informed. Keep your voice down he would be told. The neighbours. Bugger the neighbours he would inveigh, whereupon he would be dragged inside to receive a piece of his wife's mind in a less public manner.

But such bust-ups rarely interfered with a child's sense of personal control over the street and the games played there. Each child naturally made allies with friends in order to wage war on other children (not necessarily life-long enemies), or to join in competition against them, or simply to pursue activities that could not be accomplished alone. Comradeship patterned the children's play and tradition gave it substance. In addition to the games that had always existed in the area - sometimes with subtle variations between two streets separated only by a few yards - and that had been passed on from one generation of children to the next complete with rules, steps, movements, melodies, and words, there were similar well-established expectations about Christmas presents. The boys and girls of Riverside understood poverty well enough not to hope for gleaming, expensive toys and the latest costly craze in fashion; rather they asked for - and received - a more traditional set of presents. Bicycles, toy guns, dollies, train sets, and hard-wearing 'Dinky' cars all satisfied the hopes of the children whose presents would be brought out onto the streets themselves and proudly displayed. While many of the street-games simply called for the use of a ball or a skipping rope, the presents received at Christmas often led to the children becoming immersed in finding heroic routes through the cracks in the pavement for their buses and lorries and cars. Moreover, plastic kits of World War II spitfires or any other planes assembled on Christmas Day had to be flight tested as soon as possible, which meant children having to mount daring missions past mountainous window sills to the accompaniment of the sounds of screaming engines - much to the annoyance of those indoors trying to read or to do other completely boring things, such as listening to the Queen's Speech.

The children playing now in Granall Street were looking forward to receiving many of the sorts of presents David had been given as a child, and there was much confidence among certain of the boys and girls that they would be proudly riding bicycles, new or second-hand, on the morning of Christmas Day...no matter what the weather might be like. Some of the older children would stay up late on Christmas Eve to look out through their bedroom windows and listen for the ships' sirens at midnight, which would be sounded by any boats tied up along the river and the estuary.

The group of children whom David had told off earlier decided to venture to Smelly Park and to play ball tag on the big slide. A few of the girls were a bit unsure about this plan since the boys always jumped off the top of the slide into the sand-pit when they were being chased, which made it very difficult for any of the girls to hit them with the ball. And whenever one of the boys was 'on it', he'd always throw the tennis ball really hard so that it left round red marks on the girls' legs and backs. Even so, they decided to tag along provided the boys promised faithfully not to be too rough. They duly promised, but the boys' faces were full of knowing smiles and secret winks to their like-minded friends.

On their way along the street the children passed front room windows with decorations or with small Christmas trees clearly in view. But the front room where Old Man Morgan had lived was cold and bare, and the damp was beginning to take hold of the floorboards. They skipped past Mary O'Flaherty's house from where Peety Malone emerged with a note and some money to buy groceries at Joneses, the shop on the corner. The children shouted 'Pull Peety!', and Peety spun round and gunned them all down. When they had recovered, Peety asked them where they were going, and they told him and said he was to come along, especially the girls who knew he couldn't throw straight for toffee, and Peety said he'd join them after he was back from his errand. As the appointment was sealed outside the O'Flaherty's front door, they all heard Dec telling Mary to go easy on the bandit because they had to have some cash left to spend over Christmas, and Mary replying 'shut up you ol' fuss pot'. And the boys and girls all laughed, and the boys even threw the tennis ball to the girls to catch.

One of the girls dropped the ball to a chorus of butter fingers from the boys and it rolled along the gutter until it was stopped by Plod who was inclined against a lamp post and was waiting for a mate to return home with some stuff he wanted Plod to shift. Plod bent down to pick up the ball and absentmindedly threw it back to the children; he was wondering what sort of stuff his friend would want him to handle and how soon he would be able to turn it into cash in his pocket.

Plod's throw was too strong and the ball sailed over the heads of the group and with one bounce landed in the porch of Flo Roberts's house and, according to Sod's Law, which is recognized by all children, instead of bouncing back out again, it proceeded to roll into the living room. Flo was sat in front of the fire when the ball made its unannounced entrance. She was so startled she almost dropped the hand mirror with which she was inspecting the rollers in her hair. She was going up town later on and the last thing she wanted now were these bloody distractions. Flo turned to Elaine and told her to chuck the ball out, but Elaine had not even noticed the ball come in far less her mother's impatient call. Flo realized that lately Elaine had been terribly moody but instead of adopting a more sympathetic approach, Flo became infuriated by her daughter's apparent refusal to do as she was told. She was on the point of hurling the mirror at Elaine when Gran Roberts came into the room. In a soft but insistent voice she told Flo to be quiet. As Flo returned her attentions to the mirror Gran Roberts took the ball out to the waiting children and then she sat next to Elaine at the table and, taking her hand in hers, she tried to work out what it was that Elaine found so upsetting. But she never did fathom it.

The children said thank you politely to Gran Roberts and ran in a flowing huddle down Granall Street towards the park. At the bottom of the road, they saw two policemen striding purposefully in the direction of Ribley Street and the children gave them a wide berth and carried on their way full of laughter and anticipation.

CHAPTER ELEVEN

It was the middle of the afternoon when Jean Evans responded to the firm knock and found two police officers on her door step. Her fears that someone had told the police about the little disagreements, as she called them, between herself and Charlie were only partly allayed when the burly sergeant asked in a kindly manner if Mr. Hawkins were in. They disappeared completely, however, when he told her that it was about club business and would only take a minute if they could come inside. Jean admitted sergeant Hopkins and PC Marsh to the front room and complimented herself on the fact that, having just finished all the cleaning and polishing, it really did look nice and tidy. The two policemen stood awkwardly in the centre of the room taking in their surroundings until Jean asked them to sit down while she went to fetch Charlie. They took off their helmets, folded their gloves into them, unbuttoned their overcoats, and made themselves so comfortable that on her return Jean felt forced to offer them a cup of tea and a selection of biscuits, which were gratefully accepted.

Sergeant Hopkins noted that everything was very spick and span, which struck him as odd for he had Charlie down as a right slob. Still, he mused, there's no telling what lengths a woman will go to to keep a chap happy, even a man like Hawkins. He wondered whether the young constable with him was drawing any inferences from his own observations, and then the sergeant concluded somewhat wistfully that PC Marsh was probably only waiting for his tea. He made a mental note to instruct the lad in the art of keeping his wits about him and always being on the lookout for things that didn't fit - like the full case of whisky tucked behind the settee. Why would Hawkins put it there, he pondered? No room elsewhere, or off the back of a lorry maybe? The young pup hasn't even noticed it I bet, thought sergeant Hopkins. Yes, he really would have to take him in hand and buck his ideas up a bit for the lad's own good.

Charlie Hawkins came into the room and sat down without acknowledging the police officers. Funny business, thought the sergeant. Maybe there's more to this whisky than meets the eye; still, first things first. Jean Evans came in almost immediately afterwards and handed the three men their cups of tea from a brightly coloured tray with a picture of birds of paradise on it, and then she offered them each a choice of biscuits from a tin. When she had completed her hospitality duties she made to sit down, but Charlie told her sourly that she could leave, which she did immediately.

-Got some bad news for you, I'm afraid, began the sergeant when he had put his tea cup on the floor by the side of his seat.

-Oh? responded Charlie. What's it about?

-I believe that the treasurer of the Coronation Road Working Men's Club is a (the sergeant took out his notebook and consulted it momentarily) Mr. Tony Newbold.

-Yeah, that's right, said Charlie.

-To put it bluntly your treasurer has absconded with club funds.

-Has what?

-He's done a bunk, sir, with your money.

Charlie slouched alarmingly in the chair. This was bad news especially before Christmas and he knew that the situation would require careful handling if it were not to reflect badly on his responsibilities as chairman.

-The Christmas club money, Charlie blurted out.

-Gone sir. All gone, and this week's takings from the bar, added the sergeant. How much was that constable?

-Well, according to Mr. Rhys when he counted and bagged the money, there was just under two hundred and fifty pounds, said PC Marsh.

Charlie reeled under the blow. How could this be he asked himself, but the sergeant already knew what was going through the mind of chairman Hawkins.

-It was the takings that made the girl at the bank suspicious, sergeant Hopkins started to explain. Mr. Newbold drew out the Christmas Club money...

-Several hundred pounds, cut in PC Marsh who immediately fell silent after a swift look from his superior.

-He drew out the money around noon, telling the girl on the counter that it was needed to pay everyone out later today.

-But that's not till tomorrow, cried Charlie whose exasperation was steadily mounting.

-Yes, I'm coming to that sir, said the sergeant who did not like the flow of his narrative to be interrupted.

-The girl who served him at the bank thought nothing of it, continued the sergeant, but then Mr. Newbold did a silly thing. After closing the Christmas Club account, he handed over several bags of silver and coin and told the girl it was the club's takings. But instead of the money being entered as usual in the club's paying-in book when she had counted it, Newbold asked her to exchange the coin for fivers, which he pocketed along with the cash from the savings club and then he left the bank.

Charlie looked stunned, while in contrast the young constable assumed a rather bored air - he felt he had no further role to play now that his sergeant had shut him up, and he began to wish he had another cup of tea.

-Well, to her credit, the lass thought there was something suspicious and went and told the manager, said the sergeant. Of course, he immediately checked with the club and learnt that the Christmas Club funds were being paid out tomorrow not today. The steward wasn't in the club when the manager called but Mrs. Rhys was able to inform him the amount that should have been paid in was much larger than the coin Newbold exchanged, so he's obviously got cash in pound notes and fivers as well.

-Why didn't the steward pay in the takings himself? asked Charlie.

-Because he was waiting for a dray delivery and Newbold has paid in for him in the past and everything has always been perfectly in order. He is the treasurer of your club, the sergeant reminded Charlie.

-Treasurer! Bloody thief more like! Where is he now?

-After the bank manager contacted us, we thought it best to pop around to Mr. Newbold's address to sort out any misunderstandings.

-Misunderstandings! said Charlie.

-Well, it might have been a genuine mix up. But we found no sign of Mr. Newbold at his home, but the neighbours told me that they'd seen him around one o'clock this afternoon getting into a taxi with his wife and carrying a couple of suitcases.

-He's skipped it, chipped in the PC eager to contribute something now that it was clear no second cuppa was on the way.

-It very much looks like it Mr. Hawkins, said the sergeant taking a last sip of his tea. A neighbour told us that the family had found it hard going with Mr. Newbold out of work and we were advised to make enquiries at the pawnbrokers up the road from Newbold's. We duly did so, and we discovered that he had pawned several electrical goods and personal items in the shop.

-Where's the thieving git now?

-We are making further enquiries, intimated the sergeant but without giving any details. However, I must ask you to come to the club and to check the petty cash box to which I believe you and Mr. Newbold have keys.

-He may have taken money from there too, said the PC.

-The bastard! If I lay my hands on him...

-That won't be necessary Mr. Hawkins. But if we could just go and check at the club, we'd be grateful to you sir.

-Very well sergeant. Give me five minutes will you?

-Yes sir. If you don't mind, we'll go ahead if we may and meet you at the club. We have to take a statement from the steward.

-Fine, said Charlie. I'll join you soon.

As Charlie opened the door to let out the two officers, Jean reappeared and joined them in the porch. She listened intently as Charlie told her about Tony Newbold. It was only then, with the daylight catching Jean's face, that sergeant Pete Hopkins was certain that the tinge of yellow about her cheeks and the hint of puffiness, which he had glimpsed earlier, were the remains of faded bruises. Charlie finished his explanation and told Jean to run some water in a bowl for him so that he could wash and shave and then to fetch his coat from upstairs.

-I'll see you down the club in a few minutes, said Charlie to the departing officers.

-Sorry to bring you such bad news, said the sergeant. But I see you've got a good stock of whisky to enjoy over Christmas.

-Yeah, said Charlie with a weak smile.

-Oh, and I hope your missus doesn't have any more nasty accidents. Her face must have looked quite bad at one time.

-She... she fell, stammered Charlie.

-Let's hope she'll be more careful next time...if you take my meaning, said the sergeant in a cold manner. See you shortly then sir?

-Yeah, I'll be along.

Charlie went back inside. He thought of getting hold of Jean to see if she had said anything to the coppers about the whisky or the other thing. But naw, she wouldn't say anything. She knew nowt about the whisky from the guy at work. Course, it was off the back of a lorry but the coppers couldn't prove that. The sergeant was just flying a kite. And the other matter; Jean would keep stumm on that score - she knew what was best for her, did Jean. He was just a blundering copper with a kid in tow he was trying to impress. Forget it, thought Charlie. Now that he had satisfied himself on personal matters Charlie turned his attention to Tony Newbold and the money. There would be a lot of pissed-off people at the club, he thought. But he couldn't deny that the disappearance of the treasurer suited him well. The club could always get another, and he could demand more control to stop a similar thing happening again. He had never liked that flash bastard Tony in the first place. And here was a chance to fix the steward too; the stupid sod should never have let Tony take the club's money to the bank. Yeah, he could get him for that. The only thing he had to avoid was people saying the club was badly run, and that this was an example of it; he didn't want anyone criticising his job as chairman. It was nothing to do with him as chairman if the treasurer ran off with club funds. He'd find someone else to blame for that. But although he convinced himself he could weather any storm, Charlie felt angry that his authority might be called into question and he had had just about enough of those holier-than-thou coppers.

Peety Malone had finished his errand for Mary O'Flaherty and was ambling along on his way to the park to join the other children. He was quite looking forward to a game of ball tag even though he sometimes became confused about which hand to use to throw the ball. He generally used the hand with which he picked up the ball, though equal measures of mirth emerged from the children no matter which hand he employed. Not having a ball with him to practise his throwing, Peety started to draw his gun with each hand in turn to see which was the fastest and slickest. He had just arrived by the alleyway, which led to the rear entrance of the club, and was in his gunslinger's crouch poised to draw with his left hand, when Charlie Hawkins came into view. Instinctively, Peety swivelled towards the figure that had so suddenly appeared and drew against him. He shouted 'blam', but still the figure came on, so Peety caught him with a shot from the other hand this time. Instead of drawing himself or clutching his chest and crying 'Oh God, you got me' and then falling over or staggering away - as Peety's usual opponents did - this mean-looking hombre just kept on coming. Then, just as Peety was too perplexed to draw anymore, he saw too late that the man had raised his arm and was obviously going for his gun. Peety tried to get his hand out of the coat pocket that served as a holster but the dude was too quick for him. He was about to rehearse his own version of 'you dun got me you critter' - for Peety was a fair man who instinctively recognized if he'd been outgunned - when Charlie Hawkins's fist caught Peety high up on the side of his face and sent him crashing to the pavement.

Peety lay quietly on the wet paving stones. There was a puzzled look on his face, which slowly changed to one of pain and anguish, and then he began to cry; a soft insistent weeping as if he were saying goodbye to someone for ever. Two boys playing three-and-in nearby interrupted their game and came over to Peety and helped him to his unsteady feet. One of them started to upbraid Charlie who immediately lunged at the boy and threatened to give him the same bunch-of-fives he'd handed out to Peety for his insolence. The boy had easily skipped away from Charlie while his friend shepherded Peety a little distance up the street away from the ugly threats of the bully. Charlie was still threatening the remaining boy, who was prancing about just out of Charlie's range with his tongue stuck out and calling Charlie a prat and a bugger, when the front door of the Rhys's home opened.

-I can't seem to leave you alone for a few minutes without some misfortune befalling you, said the sergeant sarcastically as he filled the porch with his dark uniformed presence.

-Cut that language son, said the PC from behind his sergeant, but the boy ignored him and continued to berate Charlie.

-Thanks Tom, said the sergeant turning towards the room. We shouldn't need to trouble you again now that we've got your statement. No, you stay there and rest; we'll see ourselves out.

As the sergeant emerged onto the pavement the boy stopped his antics and ran over to join Peety and his friend.

-Bastard kids! said Charlie in a fluster.

Charlie turned and made to go through the alleyway but sergeant Hopkins told him to wait. He nodded to the constable as if to tell him he was to be sure Hawkins obeyed his command. Then he strolled quietly towards Peety and the two children. He found a handkerchief in one of Peety's pockets and encouraged him to wipe away the tears. When Peety was able to speak the sergeant listened carefully to what he had to say, and very occasionally he asked the two boys what they had seen of the incident. When he had heard enough, he put his arm around Peety and with his free hand the sergeant pulled out a small bag of sweets and gave it to him. Peety was delighted to find they were acid drops - his favourites by chance - but he was still more than willing to share them with his two friends. Sergeant Hopkins asked the elder of the two boys to make sure Peety got home safely, and then in a friendly tone he told them all to cut along.

-Righto constable, you wait for me inside the club, said the sergeant when he returned. Well off you go lad! he added brusquely when he saw his colleague hesitate.

-Look sergeant...began Charlie Hawkins.

-Shall we go through? interrupted sergeant Hopkins. After you sir, he said and beckoned Charlie to enter the alleyway.

No sooner had Charlie done so than the sergeant closed the door so that no one could see them from Granall Street nor from the yard, which was empty now that PC Marsh had entered the club as instructed. Charlie's first intimations of fear occurred the moment the door had closed and the alleyway had become quite dark. His nervousness increased as the large shadowy outline of the policeman approached him unhurriedly yet with an unmistakable menace.

-Oh don't wet yourself, said the sergeant. I'm not going to wallop you like you did poor Peety just now.

Charlie started to protest but the policeman cut him short.

-Shut it! I don't want to hear any excuses. Now listen you fat slob, I'm going to give you some good advice and you'd better take it because I shan't be saying it again. In fact, my old son, when we leave yere it'll be like it never happened.

Charlie shifted uncomfortably but he knew that to try to move away would prove to be a painful mistake.

-You ever, ever, lay a hand again on Peety, or the kids in the street, and while I'm at it, if you ever knock your missus about again, I'll be down on you like a ton of bricks. Your fat arse won't even touch the floor. Savvy?

Charlie nodded.

-Can't hear you, said the sergeant.

-I got the message, said Charlie finally in a small voice.

-That wasn't too bad was it? Now we've got that little matter sorted out, I think we should go and see about your treasurer, don't you sir?

-Pint of bitter? David Rhys asked the young PC.

-No better not; not on duty in the middle of the afternoon.

-Only drink our beer when you're nights, is it? teased David.

The constable smiled easily; he was beginning to feel more confident about his job but fathoming the ways of his sergeant could sometimes be beyond anyone.

-I wouldn't say no to a packet of crisps mind?

-Don't they feed you in the bloody police?

-We haven't had a chance to stop for anything what with going to the bank, checking Newbold's address and the pawnbrokers, and then coming yere.

-Okay, okay, point taken, said David as he threw the police officer a packet of salted crisps.

-Thanks. I hope the sarge isn't going to be all day; the chip shop's closing in a bit.

-Where is he? asked Pat Rhys who also informed the constable that he still hadn't paid for the crisps.

-Upstairs with your chairman checking the petty cash box, replied the PC fishing in his pocket for the right change.

-Yere they come now, said David who had first heard the sergeant and the chairman coming down the stairs and then had seen them pass the serving hatch at the back of the bar.

-I'll bloody swing for 'im, the light-fingered bastard, said Charlie Hawkins as he and the sergeant approached the counter.

-How much is missing? asked Pat.

-The bloody lot! That's another fair few bob our marvellous treasurer has made off with.

-Do you know where he's gone? enquired David of the sergeant.

-Not really son. We're trying to check the addresses of some of Newbold's relatives but we don't hold out much hope on that score. Still, you never know.

-Never mind, I expect the insurance will cover it, said Pat to no one in particular.

-Insurance! exploded Charlie. That's not the point! He shouldn't have been able to lay his money-grabbing hands on any of it.

Charlie's angry gaze was fixed on Pat, but she was not one to be intimidated by the blusterings of mere titty men or even club chairmen.

-Not allowing the club treasurer to handle the club's money would certainly be a novel approach to running this place, Pat replied in a measured tone.

-He should never have been given the club's takings to bank, cried Charlie.

-Don't talk so far back, said Pat dismissively. It's true Tom normally banks them himself, but Tony had done it for him several times before. What was Tom to do? Ask him if he intended to pay them in or to run off with the takings and the Christmas Club money? You're talking stuff and nonsense man.

-Always sticking up for 'im, aren't you? countered Charlie who felt the bile rising within him. Always thinking no one else but your precious husband knows the first thing about running this club. Always going on...

-There's no need for this now sir, interrupted the sergeant. I'm sure the steward can answer all your enquiries satisfactorily; there's no point in arguing with his wife, is there?

David stood to one side of his mother and saw the contempt that Charlie had for them all. Hawkins was full of more slime than the cellar, thought David who wanted to feel his fist crashing into the chairman's jaw and then, as he imagined him staggering away, to land another, which would penetrate deep into his overflowing gut and knock all the slime and shit out of him.

-This is club business, and nothing to do with you. Where is the old fart anyway? shouted Charlie as he leant over the counter so that he seemed to be spitting in Pat's face.

Pat began to say that her husband had gone to the house because he felt unwell but she was suddenly knocked aside by David. Before Charlie or the two policemen could react, David looped his arm around the back of the chairman's neck and held him firmly. In the next instant, David gripped a swathe of Charlie's lank hair with his other hand and jerked the chairman's head downwards so that his face smashed into one of the slop-dishes on the counter. The two policemen immediately moved forward and amid the cries from Pat, who was urging David to let Hawkins go, they tried to release David's hold. But Charlie's hair and neck were held with all the fury David could muster and he yanked the chairman's head to one side so that part of Charlie's face was submerged in the slops. Swiftly, David jammed his head next to Charlie's upturned ear while still holding the struggling man where he wanted him.

-I'll let you up when we've finished our little chat, said David directly into Charlie's ear.

His mother still pleaded with him to let Hawkins go, but the two policemen now stood off to await developments. The club had gone completely quiet and every face there turned to watch the drama, to gawp at the chairman twisted grotesquely across the counter, and to speculate silently what might happen next.

-You ever call my father that name again and it'll be me swinging for you. I don't like the way you talk about my father, I don't like the way you talk to my mam, and I can't see why you think you're so much better than us when you're just a piece of shit. A fat, useless, piece of shit who should mind what he says.

Charlie spluttered and tried to speak, but his mouth was pressed too firmly against the dark liquid in the tray for him to make any sense. David drew back his head and shoulders slightly but did not release his grip. Instead, even though the chairman tried desperately to break away, David slowly twisted Charlie's head from side to side so that his face passed completely through the slop tray.

-That's enough now son, said a voice. Let him go. He's not worth anymore.

With the grip suddenly released Charlie fell back and onto the floor. David turned and saw his father whose face was drawn and grey. He looked frail. The PC helped the chairman to his feet who was trying to wipe away the dregs of beer from his face and neck with a dirty grey handkerchief.

-You fucking maniac! screamed Charlie at David.

-I think you've already been warned about your language sir, said the sergeant sternly.

Charlie stared at the policeman in some disbelief; this was his club; people followed his commands here. What the hell was going on? he thought to himself.

-Are you just going to stand there? asked Charlie.

He turned with his arms splayed out wide as if appealing for justice to the whole club.

-Arrest the bastard! commanded the chairman.

-As you've already informed me sir, said the sergeant slowly, this is club business. It's none of ours.

Charlie stepped back a few paces and threw his handkerchief to the floor as a mark not so much of his rage, though that was still undoubtedly burning fiercely within him, as of his feeling of intense frustration.

-This bastard assaults me in full view of everyone and you tell me it's club business.

-Don't you think you'd be better off going home and calming down? asked the sergeant with a hint of command in his voice.

-Well, I'll tell you what's club business, said Charlie ignoring the sergeant's proposal. There'll be a committee meeting toot bloody sweet over this little lot and I'll have the lot of 'em sacked. Sacked! Do you hear me? Sacked! No one treats Charlie Hawkins like that. No one!

-As I say sir, that's club business.

CHAPTER TWELVE

It was just as well that Flo Roberts had not seen the blow Charlie Hawkins landed on Peety for she would have been off her stool and across the street to sort out Charlie herself. But Flo had been still inside trying to do something with her wilfully unmanageable hair. She had heard about the incident a while later through the street grapevine, and she had put it down to just another example of men being childish and brutal at the same time. It was a combination she had encountered all too frequently; many men were very good at it. Still, she mused, as she combed her dark, tangled hair into some semblance of acceptability, it was lucky for ol' Hawkins that she hadn't caught him doing it. Flo had no fear of men - contempt sometimes, pity occasionally, even affection now and then, but never fear - for she knew them too well even when they were cutting up rough on her. She made a mental note to give Charlie a piece of her mind the next time she saw him, and then Flo devoted her whole attention to putting on the thick black mascara around her eyes.

Flo was on a promise for that evening having arranged to see a lorry driver up town whom she had met the night before. It was late when he'd bowled into the pub but, before long, he and Flo had got talking and just after kicking out time they were in the back of his cab getting down to business. Flo paused from running the brush along her eyelashes to remember that Jim, which was the name he'd given her, had been very decent because he had paid her quite handsomely for their quick coupling. But it was always easy work with a punter like him because he had just wanted straight sex and he hadn't been all tanked up with booze, which makes some guys violent or prone to outpourings of self-pity. With the violent ones Flo could at least hit the bastards back, but there was little she felt able to do with those men whose urges drove them to find sexual release and who then dwelt, full of guilt, on the sordidness of their meaningless union. What's more, while the louts might hit her because of some perceived fault in the service she provided, those absorbed in themselves didn't give a fuck about Flo in any way at all - she was just a receptacle into which they came off.

But Jim had been none of these; just an ordinary guy away from his missus looking for a quick shag with no complications. And if some hold-up over parts meant he was staying another night that was Flo's good fortune. He did have a handsome cock too, thought Flo. Yes, she was going to have an easy time tonight. Flo spat once more on the brush and put on a final layer of 'Max Factor' black cake mascara. Having finished her make-up with an application of glossy red lipstick and a liberal covering of face powder, she pulled on her dress - the black woollen one because it was easier to lift off and wouldn't crease as much as the cotton outfit she had on the night before. Then she checked her handbag and made sure she had a supply of johnnies; there was not much money in her purse but she was confident that would be taken care of soon after meeting Jim in the Wig and Gown at 8 o'clock.

The Coronation Road Working Men's Club and Institute was packed and the blue smoke, suspended evenly throughout the room, formed a veil as thick as net curtains. In the early evening Thomas Rhys had come up from the house to serve behind the bar but the acrid smoke brought on renewed bouts of coughing and made his head spin even more. Pat and David had little difficulty in persuading him to return home with the argument that he should rest now to be ready for the real Christmas rush in a few days' time. Thomas felt sufficiently awful to accept this reasoning with little protest - he knew full well his son could cope with most things that might crop up - and as he walked through the club on his way to the house his face was so drained of colour that many of the members commented upon it.

The whole club was buzzing with the news of what had happened to the chairman that afternoon. There was no concert nor bingo that night, but even so Charlie Hawkins was expected to be in the club as usual. He never came. Charlie believed that his immediate purpose was best served simply by leaving the Rhyses to wallow in what he saw as a mess of their own making; but it turned out to be a mistake on his part. Charlie had arrogantly assumed that when the committee met, its members would endorse his threat to sack the steward and his wife with little or no opposition. However, even Alf Smith had been heard to remark in the club that evening that he thought Charlie was going too far. Moreover, Steve Curtis, who had recently heard rumours about goings-on between Charlie and his wife and was therefore in the mood to kick the chairman in his metaphoric balls, had approached some of the other committee men to try to put a stop to this nonsense, as he called it. In addition, versions of the conflict between David and Charlie, which now swept through the club in ever more graphic detail, tended to portray David not only as the wronged party, but also as a rather stylish winner - an impression strengthened by the fact of Charlie's absence.

The male members of the club could stomach the dictatorial chairman when he bossed everyone around in the name of running the place, but they were quick to spot and condemn any taint of cowardice, to which many of them attributed Charlie's non-attendance. The women in the club based much of their assessment on more sentimental considerations, such as you did not go around sacking people just before Christmas. Moreover, since the segregation rules in the club had been relaxed with the approach of Christmas, the views of both men and women in their different ways mutually reinforced the growing opinion that the chairman was getting a little too big for his boots. There were also more self-interested reasons common to all the membership that fuelled opposition to the idea of getting rid of the steward. Who would actually run the club over the festive season? In addition, some of those members who had seen how ill Thomas looked took the view that the chairman was trying to kick a man when he was down for no better reason than the man's son had put one over him. Several people began to say that the argument between the chairman and the steward's son was a private matter and that the club ought not to be dragged into it. Indeed, one or two chaps as they were served their pints by David actually congratulated him for teaching Hawkins - as they called him - a lesson. But with the exception of these few comments, the murmur of speculation and opinion, which spread like ripples throughout the members, was retained within the smoked-filled room and did not filter through to David and Pat as they served behind the bar. Before the night was out a consensus had emerged that the whole affair would blow over, but for Pat a secret dread seemed almost to be upon her family, and for David there was the growing feeling that he had been a fool and had doomed them all.

The Wig and Gown was one of those pubs with two faces. During the day the dark-suited, respectable middle classes from the law courts opposite came in for salad and quiche and Gilbey's gin. The heavy, ornately carved, woodwork of the bar reminded them of familiar surroundings and was a proper dignified sign of their own worth. The solicitors, barristers, and officials of the criminal justice system who imbibed here admired the fine old prints on the walls of the Courts of Assize, and of previous Lord Chief Justices. Like the selection of boxed cigars on show behind the bar, the decor was solid and refined; the kind of place where professional people could meet to discuss the events of the morning and to swap important items of personal information without having to rub shoulders with the inarticulate and grubby individuals whose habitual indiscretions were daily set before the courts for such professionals to process.

In the evening, however, the clientele changed. The furled umbrellas and the pince-nez departed and were replaced by travellers and reps fed up with the dull wallpaper in their pretend posh hotels up the road, and by a selection of the town's self-employed big mouths who came to the pub to lord it over the poor sods who slogged up the motorway every day and to feel they were every bit as good as, if not better than, the wigged lah-di-dahs from the court. Flo, still optimistic even as the time slipped well past 8 o'clock, had had a taste of them all anyway and there wasn't much to choose between them, except that the big-wig lawyers always tried to let on they were doing her the favour.

Flo was perched on a high stool across from the entrance where she could see everyone coming in and, more to the point, everyone could see her. The barman made a point of picking up her empty glass and hovered over her waiting for Flo to buy another or to leave. Though she had barely enough money to do so Flo asked for another gin and sweet Martini, which the barman grudgingly supplied. It was almost nine thirty and Jim wasn't coming. Flo shrugged and lifted the glass to her lips where the heady smell of gin wafted to her nostrils and the sweet, almost sickly, taste of the vermouth lingered on her tongue. Her slow swallow was interrupted by the arrival of Percy Davies, he of Percy R. Davies Scrap Metal Merchants Ltd. Percy immediately came over to Flo and sat on a stool next to her.

-Usual for me Bob and whatever Flo yere is having. How are you me darling? asked Percy in a voice rather louder than it might have been as he threw a fiver on the counter for the barman to pick up.

-Can't complain Percy old sport. Cheers!

Flo polished off her own drink and then raised the one bought by Percy in a salute to her benefactor.

-How's business then? asked Flo.

-Bloody marvellous! The best thing that ever happened to me was the closing of the Sceptre Works. There's so much scrap there it'll keep me going for ages, said Percy as he fingered his portly sides as if to reassure himself that his new wealth was as solid as his midriff.

-Silver lining in every cloud, said Flo quietly.

-What's that?

-All the guys out of work but you doing well; it's like a silver lining to...

-Oh yes, see what you mean, Percy interjected.

He sipped his whisky and water and seemed to eye Flo through the bottom of his glass. She was a good laugh, he thought to himself. She liked a good time that was for sure. Maybe he could give her a good time right now.

-Mind, a lot of these guys on the dole don't want a job. There's plenty of work at my place but can I get the beggars to work when I want them? Can I hell as like!

-P'raps you should pay 'em more, joked Flo weakly who had heard it all before from the mouths of the self-made, self-important, selfish self-employed.

-I'm not a bloody charity, you know Flo.

Percy paused for a few seconds as if weighing up his options. Flo was toying with her empty glass; she wanted another. Well, why not? he thought. They went back a long time, and he had always enjoyed their occasional meetings. It had been somehow exhilarating to hear from Flo how bad things had become in Granall Street now that he no longer lived there. But he had been told that story many times before, he reminded himself, and Flo would just trot out the same old complaints. You never dirtied on your own doorstep, he remembered his father telling him. But his doorstep was now far removed from the grime of Riverside. There was only one thing to do with a tart like Flo, Percy decided, and that was to give her a good seeing to.

-How's business yourself? said Percy leaning conspiratorially on his stool towards Flo.

-Been stood up, she answered in a matter-of-fact way.

-Maybe I could stand in for him?

-You serious Percy? said Flo.

It was not that she was surprised - nothing men did surprised her anymore - but she needed to know where she stood. Was she going to turn a trick or not, and if not, she'd have to be off to look elsewhere?

-Straight up, said Percy who held up his hands a body width apart as if to prove his fidelity in this matter.

-You got your car? asked Flo getting down to business.

-Yes, said Percy but with reluctance. It's too bloody new to be messing up the back seat, he explained but he was really worried that they might leave a stain his wife would discover.

-What about a hotel then?

-Give over Flo, I'm not made of money, you know.

Flo did not press the point for she knew that what Percy had really meant was that she wasn't worth the expense of an hotel room. She resigned herself to a knee-trembler up some back alley; it was better than nothing and at least she would have money in her purse.

-C'mon, she said. I know a place across the road.

The imposing entrance to the court building was large and, more to Flo's design, was full of deep shadows. As soon as she and Percy had arrived and made sure no one was close by, Flo had hitched up her dress and unzipped Percy.

-Jesus mother of god! It's cold! said the punter but Flo had already taken his flaccid cock in hand and was beginning to pump some life into it.

-Just slip this on there's a good boy, murmured Flo now that Percy had acquired the right dimensions.

-Bugger off, I'm not sticking my dick into a fucking sack, protested Percy.

-It'll be extra, said one business person to another.

-I'll give you extra, breathed Percy into Flo's ear as he gripped her shoulders and roughly entered into her, bending at the knees and then straightening his legs for each thrust.

-There's something extra for you. Do you like that eh? Do you like it? I bet you do.

Flo jerked upwards under each attack, and she was conscious of her woollen dress catching on the stonework behind her. She held her arms around Percy's back and tried to look interested. But it was difficult to let out moans of delight when being done over in such an unsubtle fashion. And that's what they wanted, of course - groans and breathless moans to tell them yes, you're the best, the biggest, the best, the absolute...oh God, oh God, I'm coming... best. But with some men Flo couldn't do it, and Percy was one of those; the kind of man to whom Flo would just cling while he got on with it and every now and then she would give him an encouraging ooh and ah, but not too many in circumstances such as these or he might start thrusting so hard that the stonework would be ground smooth with the force of Flo's arse going up and down along it. Yes, thought Flo, Percy was only worth an occasional ooh.

Her back became sore under the weight of Percy's thrusts but he continued to bang away and to mutter all manner of things in Flo's ear to which she had long ceased to listen. Quite possibly he could keep this up for some while, reflected Flo ruefully. Her attention was taken by the coat of arms over the court entrance and the Latin inscription, which she could not decipher. Bloody high and mighty so-and-so's, thought Flo. They always think they're right, the people that work here. Even when Flo appeared on charges of soliciting, it was like she was guilty from the word go, like they had her down as once a tart always a tart. But on one occasion, she showed them, she'd got the better of the snooty bastards.

It had been three years ago, and some smart-arsed copper who thought he knew it all had picked her up outside the King's Arms. Next day she was in court on a charge of soliciting. What had got up Flo's nose was the fact that she'd been arrested because it was her turn - the coppers hauled in the known pros on a sort of rota basis and gave the impression that they were combating street prostitution. In fact, they were doing bugger all about it. But on the night Flo had been arrested outside the King's Arms she had not, in fact, been looking for a punter but had simply been waiting for a bus to take her home. In court she had pleaded not guilty to the amazement of everyone, and so the police officer had to be called to give his evidence. When he had finished, a determined Flo had conducted her own defence, which amounted to only three questions. What were the contents of her handbag when she was searched at the police station? The policeman turned to the bench as if he could not believe his ears, but the chairman told him to answer the question. After consulting his notebook, the officer informed the court that the handbag contained a handkerchief, some keys, a lipstick, a powder compact, and a purse in which were two stamps and a small sum of money in coin. No johnnies? The policeman glowered at Flo and then looked again at the bench as if pleading with them to halt this macabre performance, which he found humiliating. At length he found the strength to inform their worships that no contraceptives were found in the handbag. How then could I have been soliciting? asked Flo of the policeman and the bench in a tone that fully suggested that it was physically impossible for someone of her trade to operate without the benefits of the London Rubber Company upon her person. And damn it to high heaven and back, thought Flo as Percy bounced up and down before her, when the dust had settled and the magistrates had returned from their tea and fags, they actually found her not guilty and she had walked free without having to pay the usual fine - a fine she normally paid off by satisfying more customers.

This particular customer sounded like he was very close now to being satisfied, so Flo squeezed his prick a little more tightly with her vaginal muscles and soon Percy was puffing and panting and coming.

-Ooh big boy, she whispered in Percy's direction.

-You better believe it.

When Percy had completed his transaction with Flo, he steadied himself against a stone pillar and pulled up his underpants and trousers. He searched inside his wallet as Flo adjusted her dress and thought to herself that the back of it was probably all rucked up and maybe ruined.

-Yere, this should do you, said Percy handing her a few quid.

He quickly turned around and anxiously peered out of the entrance.

-I'm off then. You can find your own way home, can't you?

-Don't worry about me. See you around.

-Yeah, see you sometime.

Percy hurried away and Flo counted the money and then put it in her purse. Stingy bastard, she thought. To cheer herself up she decided to go back to the Wig and Gown for a few more gins; she deserved them, she convinced herself.

It was gone midnight and Pat Rhys had left David to lock up while she went to the house to check on her husband. She found Thomas asleep, albeit fitfully and with a low rumbling growl punctuating his breathing, and as quietly as possible she undressed and slipped beside him under the blankets. His body felt cold but was covered in sweat. Pat snuggled against him and soon fell asleep praying for a change of fortune - just a chance to stay one step ahead of the deadly game.

David locked the door and left the smell of smoke and the odour of beery breath to dissipate as best it might. Stepping out into the yard, David was caught in the steady rain, some of which was turning to sleet, but despite the weather he stopped to check that the bottle shed was securely locked and then he went through the narrow alleyway to close the door into Granall Street. It was still and dark along the length of the terraced houses. All the people had gone to bed and they were oblivious once more for a short time of the disappointments of their own lives and the shortcomings of their own homes. Not so long ago Granall Street and the surrounding roads quickened to the pace of the steelworks and the other factories. Workers would wake up the streets before dawn as breakfasts were made and sandwiches readied and wrapped in grease-proof paper. As one shift tumbled home again via the pub and betting shop, so another wave of men set off in the afternoon. In the days when there was plenty of overtime, men were eager to take an extra few hours on the two till ten evening shift at the Sceptre plant so that even in the small hours workers moved along Granall Street and throughout Riverside as willing accomplices in tune with the needs of industry.

Then, with a savage purpose of mind, industry had decided that it no longer had need of such men and the streets became much quieter. Yes, they were all asleep in Granall Street now, and only the industrious black pats were scurrying silently through the people's homes, polluting their food, crawling into their secret places, which they thought were private and safe, and daring even to creep across their children's trusting faces. Each night an army of well-drilled cockroaches went on the march and each morning a beleaguered people tried to sluice them away or to squash such stragglers as they could find and to damn them with sullen imprecations.

The rain embraced the street with its pitter-patter and the opaline sleet partially cloaked the jagged edges of decay from David's view. Stretching into the distance on either side of the alleyway door where David stood was an uneven pavement, a grey masterpiece of interlocking cracks and crevices. At intervals beneath broken gutterings, the rain fell headlong to the pavement and swirled towards the drains where it carried along some of the muck and grime of Granall Street until the gutter itself became clogged with rubbish. But the rain never cleansed the place of the people's stoic acceptance.

David was about to lock the door when he saw a female figure stagger across the road at the top of the street. Half on the pavement and half in the gutter, the figure made her lopsided way nearer until, caught in the dim light of a street-lamp and impeded by one of the few parked cars, David was able to recognize her. It was Flo Roberts - full of the festive spirit and of the gin served at the Wig and Gown - who now began to belt out a song. Her voice and style were unmistakable, and David immediately drew back into the deep shadows of the alleyway for he had no desire at all to meet a drunk and potentially boisterous Flo. She continued to sing, out of tune, the soulless words of a mawkish song about a woman missing her man at Christmas.

It took Flo some moments to work out why she could not make any forward progress. But as soon as the penny dropped, she stopped her wailing, loudly cursed the car and the stupid prick who had left it there for her to trip over, and then gave the sorry vehicle a sound kicking. Her curses and the crash of stiletto heel on the car's fender echoed along the street, but as Flo tired of her assault she eventually found a precarious route around the offending vehicle. As Flo drew closer, David could see that her eyes were dark patches where the mascara had run and her dress was heavy and misshapen with the rain, while her coat appeared to be attached to the strap of her handbag, which she trailed behind her. With her dark hair strung along her back Flo had a witch-like quality about her.

Flo lurched a few paces beyond her front door and then lurched back again. In the tangle of coat, strap, and handbag she was unable to find her key so she began to bang on the door with her fist, and to shout for good measure that every lazy bastard asleep in the street should wake up. A window opened somewhere close by and an irate voice told the bitch to shut up and go to bed. Flo spun around suddenly so that David did not dare move - she seemed to be staring right at the alleyway but was unable to detect anyone in the darkness. The sound of the window elsewhere now being slammed shut in anger deflected Flo's attention and she spat out further profanities in that direction. David drew back a shade further into the dark recess.

Flo's door still remained obstinately closed but she was no longer capable of continuing her assault since her dirt-splattered legs had almost buckled under her. Then they gave way completely and Flo found herself falling to the pavement. In an attempt to regain her feet, she fell over again and this time her blubbery frame rolled into the water-filled gutter. As the dirty water drenched her clothes David caught sight of a movement in the upstairs window of Flo's house. The curtains were drawn completely back and the sleight figure of Elaine, who was standing on the top of her bed, was transfigured in the window frame. Her forehead was pressed against the glass so that her breath misted the pane, and her arms - resting on the frame - were stretched out to the side. As the sobbing child turned her head from side to side, David could see the highlights in her hair and the effortless beauty of her face. Not even the pain and the misery she was feeling now would prevent her soon from becoming a most desirable woman, thought David.

Beneath the window, Flo was now crawling on her hands and knees in search of one of her shoes, which lay partially submerged in the pool of water around her. Her black dress, sodden with water, was rucked up around her thighs and hung formlessly from her body. After her encounter with Percy, Flo had not bothered to replace her panties and as she searched, dog-like, for the lost article her naked arse wobbled in plain view. Flo was still floundering and cursing when David looked again at the upstairs window. It was difficult for him to be sure but it seemed that the figure now pressed close to the glass was mouthing the same words over and over again - 'Mam, oh Mam'. Even through the rain-lashed window, against which Elaine stood crucified, David could see the tears running remorselessly down her pretty cheeks and, as he turned away and locked the door, he felt they might flow forever. A few minutes later as David lay in his own bed and thought of Elaine, he heard Flo's front door open and the soft begging of Gran Roberts to her daughter to come inside. A while later everything fell quiet in the street and the only sound David heard was that of his father's ragged breathing, which rang throughout the house and amplified David's uneasiness.

CHAPTER THIRTEEN

You didn't hear her at all then last night? David asked his parents.

Pat and Thomas Rhys both indicated that they had heard not one tuneless note of Flo's song nor any of her cussing, much to David's surprise. They were all together in the front room warming themselves by the coal fire. It seemed strange to each of them to be there, for it was not yet properly Christmas when the front room might have been used to entertain relatives and friends. Normally, the room was nothing more than storage space for the hefty three-piece suite and the glass cabinet with its shelves full of small knick-knacks, miniature pottery models of dogs, and the remains of a China tea-set. But Pat had felt it best to bring Thomas out of himself by lighting a fire in the front room so that, even though he was not yet ready to return to work, he would at least not have to stay upstairs in a cold bedroom or slouch around the dreary scullery. And if he felt like a lie down, he could always put his feet up on the settee, where Pat had left several blankets in such anticipation.

-Don't fuss, said Thomas with mock exasperation as Pat brought in a couple of pillows and placed those too on the settee.

-Best to do as you're told, said David to his father in an ironic manner.

-Maybe you're right lad, responded Thomas. God knows, she's had a lot of practice telling me what to do.

-And a fat lot of notice you've taken either, said Pat as she spread out one of the blankets across the settee and removed David out her way almost with the same movement.

-There you are dad, she's bossing me about now, said David who promptly sat down again in the armchair by the fire opposite his father.

-Be serious you two! said Pat who was anxious to see to her husband's immediate needs.

-There, she said with a gesture towards the settee. You can spread out nicely now if you've a mind to.

-I'll go an' spread myself around the cellar then, mimicked David.

-No, you hang on. There's things to talk about first, Pat ordered, but not in an unkindly fashion.

-Charlie Hawkins I suppose, said David.

-Well what else? replied Pat.

-Look mam, I didn't set out to have a go at him but the truth is...

-Truth is you lost your temper and then had a go at him, said Pat rather more sternly than she had intended.

-He'll get over it, volunteered David. Anyway mam, this is between me and him really. I don't see how it involves you and dad.

-The sack! That's how it involves us, cried Pat.

-Now hold on, there's a good girl, Thomas began. There's no point in blaming the boy. He was only sticking up for us and...

-Sticking up for you more like, said Pat swiftly.

-C'mon luv, what's that matter? You, me, the three of us; it's all the same isn't it? And I seem to remember you haven't been so good in the past in keeping your temper where Charlie Hawkins is concerned.

Pat bit her lower lip and seemed awkward and distant for a while. Even when Thomas beckoned her to come and sit on the arm of his chair, she remained standing silently in the middle of the room.

-I'm sorry Dave bach, she said finally. It's not your fault and I shouldn't have gone on at you like that. It's Hawkins that's got my goat and there's no way I can hit back at him. To tell the truth, I'm scared about your dad losing his job.

-Awh, it'll not come to that mun, said Thomas.

-But what if it does Tom? What will we do? Where will we live? We'll have to leave this place, poor as it bloody-well is.

There was quiet but mounting panic in her voice, which Thomas detected immediately. He rose from his chair and embraced his wife.

-I said it won't come to that. Charlie Hawkins is not that powerful; he's not God Almighty, said Thomas.

-But he thinks he is, offered David.

-Aye maybe so, continued Thomas, but it'll take more than the likes of him to shift me and your mother.

-But what if..., persisted Pat who was cut short by her husband.

-If, and I say if, it came to being booted out, I'd get a job at another club tomorrow.

-Tomorrow? cried Pat in anguish.

-Well, you know what I mean. I'm well-known in the town and there'll be a vacancy in no time soon. But I'm trying to tell you, if you'll only listen luv, that we are not going to get sacked.

-Yes, c'mon mam, listen to dad. I can say I'm sorry to Hawkins. What can he do? He can stop me serving behind the bar in the evenings, but he's not going to be there in the early mornings or every hour of the night and day to stop me helping with the stocking up and the cellar work.

-There'll be no need to say sorry to Hawkins or to anyone else, said Thomas in a measured voice. Now, listen to me Pat. It will blow over and Hawkins can't sack me for something our son did to him.

Pat was not entirely convinced but she kissed her husband on the cheek and put on a smile for his sake. She ruffled David's hair and told him playfully that it needed cutting, as if she were confirming how sorry she was for her earlier words. And when David told her there was no chance of him having it cut, even for Christmas, she knew they were all friends again. Pat still believed that ahead lay a hard path, but now that harmony had been restored within the family, they could at least face it with a united front. Leaving the two men in front of the fire, Pat went through into the scullery to be alone with her thoughts as she prepared their meal for later.

Thomas put some more lumps of fine shiny black coal on the fire. David thought to himself that despite the pain his father had suffered over the years getting the stuff out of the ground, he didn't half like to build up a blaze.

-Not so fast young lad, said Thomas as David got up and was about to leave.

David had not been spoken to in such a manner by his father since he had been a small boy. Whenever David had been discovered upto no good, his father's essentially kindly attitude always prevented him from laying a hand on his son, so that it was only with the tone of his voice that he showed disapproval. With the expectation that he was about to receive that disapproval because of his run-in with Hawkins, David turned and stood facing his father. Thomas indicated with a wave of his arm that David should sit down again. But when he spoke there was no sign of criticism, only of the concern that a thoughtful father had for his son.

-There are a couple of things I wanted to say to you, but not in front of your mother, said Thomas as he watched the flames dance above the softly hissing lumps of coal.

-What is it dad? said David who was unsure whether he wanted to hear what his father had to tell him.

-I let on to your mam that if we had to leave yere, I'd get another club easily.

-And so you would. You've always served the best pint around, said David.

-Shush a minute David and let me finish, there's a good lad. All the good pints of beer in the world don't count for nothing when some bunch of committee men are looking you over and trying to make up their mind whether to offer you the job. It's how much hard work they think they can get out of you, that's what they're interested in.

-But dad, you always told me how important it was to serve a decent pint.

-Aye, I did that son, but the importance is not for the committee men and the club members, half of which only think they know a good pint, but for yourself. It's for your own pride in your work. If I have to go for another job, okay the committee will know I can serve good beer, but they'll see a sick man, a sick man David, and they'll think to themselves how much work can we get out of this bloke.

-There are other jobs, protested David.

-At my age and in my state of health? There's only three things I've ever known how to do well - soldiering, working as a collier, and being a club steward, and I can't go back to the first two so I have to hang on to the last one.

-Were you just letting on to mam too about it all blowing over, or do you really think Hawkins will sack you? asked David who could not bring himself to look directly at his father.

Thomas leaned forward in his chair and reached across to tap David's knee so that his son raised his head and saw the smile on his father's face.

-No, I wasn't just letting on. Hawkins isn't going to get rid of me easily and certainly not without a fight. David, I had to tell you about my chances of getting work in another club, not because I think I shall soon be out on my ear from this place, but because it's no use hiding the truth.

-So, you're not feeling too good right now, but you'll get better, said David as much trying to convince himself as to sound optimistic for his father's sake.

-Yes, I could, and that's what I hope for naturally, but I must say I can't remember when I felt worse these last few days. Anyway, that's not the issue. The issue is you and what you're going to do.

-Me? said David in surprise.

-Of course! It's your life that matters. Why do you think I've gone on about my health and the problems of finding another club?

-Well, so as I can help you and mam...

-No! Not that son. You believe that I want you to work in the club as a prop for my own inadequacies, to shore up my weaknesses.

-Dad, it's not like that at all, protested David.

-Hear me out. I'm not ungrateful, you know that lad. And listen, it's not that I'm too proud to have my son do part of the job I haven't been able to do lately. I don't want you sucked into this business; there's no future and no life in it worth having, believe me.

-But dad, you don't expect me to just walk out and leave you to it.

-I'm not saying that. Look, when they shut the works and you had nothing to do all day, I thought that involving you in the club would... well, you know... prevent idle hands... No, I don't mean getting into mischief and running foul of the law - I know you better than that - I was thinking of the loss of spirit that happens to men when they are out of work and have too much time on their hands. I saw too much of it in the valleys before the war. Mind you I was also grateful for the hand you could give me, and I could legitimately pay you a few quid for the work you did. What's the No.2 account for if not for us? laughed Thomas.

-What's changed? I don't understand, said David.

-What's changed is that I didn't realize how involved you'd become in the work at the club. I hadn't counted on being so ill but even so I felt like I've laid a trap for you.

-Don't talk so daft mun! A trap, why would you do that?

-Not on purpose, not deliberately, but it's happened all the same. You've got eyes in your head and a brain too; you know how much work lately you've had to do for me so that it's become an obligation, even a duty, as far as you're concerned.

-You're my father...and I love you.

Thomas felt the hesitation; men rarely spoke of their love for one another.

-And I love you too, and it's because I love you that I don't want you dragged down with me.

Thomas paused a moment to gaze once more into the flames and then he resumed.

-I know work in Cwmporth is not easy to find right now. Maybe there's work elsewhere and if you were interested in going after it, I don't want to be a burden to you.

David was about to protest again but his father held up his hand in a weary fashion to indicate that David should not interject.

-It sounds harsh perhaps what I've said, but I've never held the truth from you. Men often have difficult decisions to make, but they should always take them knowing the truth and not have the wool pulled over their eyes or, worse, deceive themselves because they are not strong enough to face the truth.

Both of them shifted in their chairs and the brief silence was punctuated only by the sudden collapse of a pile of coal on the fire and by Pat next door getting water from the bosh.

-You're thinking I've deceived your mother by not telling her what I've told you, said Thomas. Maybe so. Your mam's a worrier and sometimes she needs me to tell her everything's okay even when she knows it isn't. But we're a team, your mam and I, and we'll work out something between us. It's different for you.

-I'm part of the team too; it's all the same family, said David.

-Of course you are. You don't have to stay yere with us though to be part of that family. You've got your own life to lead. Listen David...all I'm trying to say is that you mustn't feel obligated to us, to me. If there's something out there, a job or whatever, that you want then go and take it. Don't hang around because you think you owe it to me to shift those fucking barrels I can't handle anymore.

-Then who'll shift them?

-Me if I get better, or I'll find someone who'll do it for a few bob. There's plenty in Granall Street alone who would like to pick up a little extra on their dole money. I'll find a way. I'm not driving you out David, I'm only saying it doesn't have to be you who does that work. You don't owe me anything son.

David sat silently for a few minutes while his father resumed his gaze into the flames. The light from the fire played across Thomas's face but not even the warm flames could disguise how drawn and tired he looked.

-Why did you leave Tredegar? asked David eventually.

His father's surprise at the question caused him to pause a moment before he answered, as if this part of his past were a slow and painful process to recall.

-It was a hard life before the war in the pits but at least there seemed a purpose to it all. I started underground when I was fourteen and I learnt a lot, most of all to depend on your fellow miner. I became known as a good collier and when I no longer had the strength and the wind to work at the coal face, it just wasn't in me to take a lesser job on top, so I left. That was pride, maybe the wrong sort, I don't know. Anyway, I ended up eventually at this club in Cwmporth, and if I had the choice over again, I think I would still have left the pit but I sure as bloody hell wouldn't have become a steward. Underground, it was each man working with his butty; here, it's small mouthy men set against each other in piffling unimportant ways. But you can't let yourself descend to that level. Take Hawkins for example. With him it's all a war of attrition. I can do without it, but I'm not going to lick his arse. Righto, I can't get at him by hitting him, like you did, but I can get back at him in my own way; by turning in a good day's work and keeping my self-respect. But it's a cruel job for all that. Stay out of it, David.

David got out of his armchair and picked up the small coal bucket by the side of the fender.

-Let me put on a few more lumps for you, said David.

-You'll have your mam on to me again for that, smiled Thomas.

-Dad...I understand what you've told me and I appreciate your concern about my future. But I don't know yet what that future will be. Until it all becomes clearer, I'm going to carry on giving you a hand; I'll know when it's time to move on. Okay?

Thomas nodded and felt glad he had got at least one thing off his chest, even if the phlegm and the gripping tautness were other matters he had not been able to remove.

-Now if you'll allow me, teased David, I'll go and do the stocking up.

As David opened the door into the scullery, he heard his father pick up the newspaper but he did not open it.

-So, you had his head in the slops tray, did you? said Thomas.

-Yes, replied David.

-Best fucking place for it too, said Thomas.

-Language Tom! called Pat without any rancour from the scullery.

Thomas was after all only referring to the worst of the titty men and so his swearing could almost be excused. He could be forgiven too, thought Pat, for talking privately man to man with his son, but then Pat had already intuitively worked out more of their conversation than either of them would have believed.

The post being pushed through the letterbox interrupted Thomas's interest in the match report. What a shame Cwmporth rugby weren't doing better, he thought, as he went to collect the few bills that had dropped on the mat in the porch. On a whim, Thomas opened the front door and stood for a few minutes peering into the street. He rarely ventured into Granall Street - or into Coronation Road for that matter - so bound was he by the demands of the club. The houses in Granall Street reminded Thomas of the terrace where he had grown up in Tredegar, except that here the streets were laid out next to one another in lines on flat ground, whereas at home the rows were stacked one above the other as they marched up the mountain. All his hard work had brought him to this - a small cell of bricks and mortar surrounding by hundreds just like it, and all of them crumbling away uncomplainingly. He thought how rich he'd be if he had a pound for every barrel in the cellar he had tapped and spiled. It was the same thought he'd nursed underground when, if he had a pound for every blow he'd struck against the coal seam with his mandril, he'd be richer still. A good collier always listened to the coal; it told him how hard he'd have to sweat. Thomas remembered that if you struck the seam with the pickaxe and the sound came back all tight, like a bell, it would be hard going to prize the coal free. But if it sounded looser, like a drum, then you knew that the coal would come easier and that you would get a fair reward for your labour. Part of that reward would be spent down the miners' welfare club where the talk was always about work, whereas in the mine itself the chat was always about sex. And could they talk. In the days before Ty-Triste had a pit-head baths, the talk in the club was so big that the colliers had to cover their pints with beermats to stop all the coal dust falling into their drinks. But, duw, it was a life.

The appearance of Peety Malone in front of the house brought Thomas's reverie to a close. It suddenly occurred to Thomas that there was too much change going on for Peety's world to remain safe and sure for much longer. There would soon be no more room nor tolerance for the village idiot. Cavie and Plod swaggered along the pavement in Thomas's direction and then passed him without acknowledgement. Why should they, he mused? They seemed to be set on going off somewhere definite, yet in their hearts and minds they were drifting aimlessly; the poor sods had even less of a place than Peety. Across the street, Mary O'Flaherty, Jean Evans and Betty Sawyer were wrapped in gossip. They were waiting for the club to open so that they could transfer the gossip to the side of the one-armed bandit.

What a dirty place it is, whispered Thomas to himself, as if his eyes were surveying Granall Street for the very first time. He felt warm inside when he thought of his son; mind, he needs a gentle push to get on though. And he felt warmer still at the thought of his wife. However would he have found the strength to go on if not for her? The dull grey street was oppressive and Thomas returned to his place inside by the fire where he located his cigarettes, lit one, and inhaled the smoke deeply. Immediately he began to cough violently. When the coughing had subsided, Thomas held the cigarette in his hand without drawing on it further and, after a few moments, he turfed it into the fire; he felt so bad that he didn't even fancy his fags anymore. He simply sat there and stared into the flames, and watched his life go up in smoke.

CHAPTER FOURTEEN

It was the morning of the 20th December 1973. Next year would be Thomas Rhys's fifty fifth birthday. Where does the time go? thought Thomas as he entered the scullery. He turned his thick and powerful wrist to look at his watch, which it took him a few seconds to bring properly into focus. Thomas had been an early riser practically every day of his life, but today he was surprised to see how late it was. By the state of the fire and the empty mugs of tea perched on the mantelpiece, it was clear that Pat and David had been up and about for some while. Thomas guessed that Pat must have gone out to the shops on Coronation Road to buy groceries and he knew full well that David would be working in the club, preparing everything for open tap.

David had just reconnected the pipes and was emerging from the cellar when his father greeted him.

-Blimey, you've not been hanging about, said Thomas when he saw that David had just finished cleaning the pumps. What time did you start?

-About 8 o'clock. There was a fair bit of stocking up to do as well, so I thought I'd get stuck into it early.

-I'll give you a hand, if you like, offered Thomas.

-Feeling a bit better then? inquired David.

-A bit. My head's a little clearer but my chest is still tight.

David was pleased that his father felt slightly better but he didn't want him rushing into things too quickly and overdoing it. He compromised by ensuring that he carried all the cases upto the bar from the shed and also helped his father to put the bottles on the shelves, choosing the most awkward places for himself to stack. When they had finished, Thomas sat on the only chair behind the bar and lit himself a cigarette.

-I'd better sort out the yard and the bottle shed, David told his father. I'll see you in a bit.

Thomas nodded and as David left, he leaned forward in his chair to peer into the cellar through the open flap door. He's done a good job and left it clean and tidy, he thought to himself as he drew long and hard on the cigarette. Immediately, Thomas began to cough and each attempt to clear the tautness in his chest seemed to scrape across the fibre of his lungs so that they burned with pain. It was as if an awful suffocating membrane were closing over his mouth and nose, starving him of air, and forcing him to try to burst the deadly bubble through the violence unleashed in every cough. His body was wrenched back and forth in the chair and his cigarette was thrown out of his grasp to the floor. Thomas's thin face became red and bloated as his tongue protruded through his dribbling lips as if seeking air on its own account. His eyes watered and seemed fit to bulge from his head such was the pressure building up within him. If only the bubble would burst, prayed Thomas. The dreadful howl of cough on cough filled Thomas's consciousness until there seemed room for nothing else, but suddenly there was added to it the quivering realization of a new pain in his chest, more vicious and more focused than any before. He tottered on the edge of the chair, which still shook under the paroxysm of harm being done to his now powerless body; he tried once more to breathe, to break the curse that had followed him most of his life, and then Thomas pitched forward and fell headlong into the cellar below.

It was a fall that, for Thomas, lasted an eternity. Even as his body bounced off the stairs and smacked into the concrete floor of the cellar, Thomas Rhys had already begun his never-ending journey to nowhere. The booming echo of the sound of his head catching against the side of one of the beer barrels had subsided and the cellar was deathly quiet. Thomas's tall body lay twisted in the passageway between the two shelves, his treacherous heart and his spent lungs now still. A few clouded drops of siliva dropped from the corner of his openly surprised mouth. Thomas was dead, caught within his prison, staying down within a new Ty-Triste.

When David returned, he assumed his father was in the gents and it was only as he made to close the flap door that he saw his body below and the ugly gash on the side of his face. David scrambled down the stairs, his own heart beating in a frantic panic for fear of the worst and his head already preparing him for it. He placed his hands underneath his father's body and lifted him around so that he was fully on his back in the cramped space and, in desperation, David tried to revive him. No breath emerged from the tortured lungs and the redundant heart did not resume. For a moment, David cradled his father in his arms and then he laid him gently on the floor of the cellar where the barrels of beer loomed large all around him.

As David looked at his father, his body seemed thinner and the hair on his head greyer. The large hands still appeared as powerful as ever, but the bent fingers were already drained and somehow fragile, as if to handle them roughly would make them break. His whole body now nestled sourly against the wet floor and in his unseeing eyes, which reflected the grey droplets hanging on the ceiling, there seemed to be a sad resignation. David kissed his father's cheek, and as he did so he knew with a crushing certainty that his father had not wanted to go this way, but the struggle had become too hard.

A few minutes ago, they had shared a life together but now a mere instant had laid waste to it all. There remained only dead flesh and memories; each man's final fall ended this way. He was already a shell, reflected David and the essence, which had been Thomas Rhys, had been destroyed in less time than it takes God or man to blink. The thought of God sneaking unbidden into David's mind made him cringe with feelings of foolishness. David no longer had any belief in God, and if he had still believed, he would surely have despised Him. God was nothing more than an embarrassing cliche; it was a word that people mouthed because they did not know otherwise how to respond. God was of no importance. The only thing that mattered now was that Thomas Rhys had died alone, and David had missed the opportunity to say goodbye to his father. There would never be another chance to greet him again. A single second had stolen him away and separated him from those who loved him by the cruelty of eternity.

A familiar world, which David had taken for granted for most of his life, had collapsed, and he reacted to it in an almost mechanical fashion as he tried to make sense of the new order of things. Although fully conscious of what had happened, David moved slowly, as if concussed, but eventually he reached the telephone behind the bar and rang for an ambulance, which he assumed would take his father away to wherever corpses go before they are returned to their families for burial. Then he locked the premises securely, so that he could be quite sure his father would be safe, and went in dread to find his mam.

CHAPTER FIFTEEN

Now the noise was no longer there, the house felt strange and they missed him all the more. Thomas's cough had for years been a familiar sound in the background; and even though it occasionally gave cause for concern, how Pat and David yearned to hear it again. In the past few weeks, as Thomas's health deteriorated, the coughing had become more strident than ever before, but now its very absence cut deeply into his loved ones, and small, matter-of-fact events provided them with unrelenting doses of fresh pain and anguish. The chair where Thomas used to doze in front of the fire in the afternoons remained bleakly empty; the last cup of tea he had enjoyed stood unmoved on the draining board by the bosh; and on the mantelshelf the pools coupon lay waiting to be completed.

-I expect him to walk in any minute, said Pat more to herself than to David.

Her eyes were red and puffy and her mind was still numb with the shock of her sudden loss. When Pat had returned to the house and David had told her what had happened, she had nearly fainted away and it was with great difficulty that David had held her up and then managed to get her to a chair. The arrival of the ambulance in the street had caused a small crowd to gather intent on finding out what was amiss. Among the people surrounding the ambulance, David had spotted Betty Sawyer and she willingly agreed to sit with Pat while David unlocked the club and accompanied the ambulance men to the cellar.

-Another cup of tea luv? asked Betty, but Pat's first cup was still untouched.

Before the arrival of the ambulance, David had tried to remove some of his father's things from the scullery in the mistaken belief that this would make matters easier for his mother, but she had told him to leave them, for she would take them herself to Thomas in a while. Uncertain yet fearful what she had meant, David had telephoned the doctor and also his relatives in Tredegar but as yet the only support available to his mother was himself and Betty.

-I still haven't wrapped Tom's Christmas present, said Pat.

She turned to Betty, as if in a daze, and asked her if she thought Mrs. Jones in the shop would have some wrapping paper.

-Course she will. There's plenty of time for that. I'll get you some myself later on, offered Betty.

-No. I should go now really, and then it'll be all nice and pretty and ready for Tom on Christmas Day.

-Why don't you stay yere now Pat? said Betty softly. David will be back soon and the doctor's on his way.

When the doctor arrived, he duly administered a sedative and Betty put Pat to bed upstairs. The doctor told David he would come back tomorrow and Betty said she would stay with Pat for the rest of the day to ensure she would be alright. David sat by the fire alone and took out his father's possessions from a brown paper bag. They amounted to a watch, a gold ring, a wallet, some loose change, and a set of false teeth. One of the ambulance men had gathered everything together and handed them to David because he said things sometimes had a habit of going missing down the hospital. He told him that the undertaker would want the teeth for when the body was laid out for burial.

David had stayed at the top of the cellar steps as the ambulance crew had checked to see if anything could be done for his father. The stairs to the bar were far too steep for the men to carry out Thomas's stretchered body, so David had then to descend and squeeze past the living and the dead in order to open the cellar flaps at the front from where the crew took Thomas out, like an empty barrel being returned to the brewery. By then word had spread throughout Granall and Ribley streets of Thomas's death and several committee men had arrived at the club. They offered their sympathies to David, enquired after his mother, and then they retired in a small huddle to confer. A few minutes later, as David was closing the flap door behind the bar, they returned to tell him that the club would not open today. They would contact him later to let him know what would happen after that. David thanked them and almost said aloud how surprised he was that they should have taken such a decision in the absence of the club chairman. But grief held his tongue and he let the matter pass, glad only that he could now return to the house to see his mother and to make arrangements for his father's funeral.

After his final escorted journey through the club, into the back yard and along the alleyway into Granall Street, where the crowd stood back silently and respectfully as Thomas's body was put into the ambulance, he had been taken to the morgue at the general hospital just outside the city centre. The undertaker had been to the house soon afterwards. He arranged for a reverend to conduct the service, and assured David that the funeral would take place before Christmas, in fact on Christmas Eve. As he put it, the people at the morgue were very good and they wouldn't want him there over Christmas anyway if they could avoid it. So, they laid Thomas's cold body on a slab and cut him up in quick time, like a piece of meat in a processing factory, and then they packed his resewn body off to the chapel of rest, after giving the cause of death as a coronary occlusion.

Pat greeted the news of the cause of death with some disdain. She did not deny that a heart attack had finished off her husband but she held to the belief that thirty years of coal dust had pretty well done the job before that. By now Pat had accepted the reality of Thomas's death and was trying to compose herself for the funeral tomorrow. She and David had spent many hours together in the last three days trying to make sense of what had happened. In between the periods when they would cling to one another and cry without stint, they would recall the funny times they had had together, or retell some anecdote that Thomas himself had been fond of narrating. And this would bring on the tears again and cause Pat to wail in despair that she was alone. Guilt would make her apologize to David - of course, she still had him - but how could you explain to a son the loss of a husband and lover? But David understood anyway and held his mother tightly and stroked her hair softly, as if she were a child, and told her everything would be fine in the end.

The club reopened the day following the steward's death and David took his place behind the bar. The committee allowed a new barmaid to be hired on a temporary basis to help out, and the club membership officially sent its condolences to the family and arranged for flowers to be sent to the funeral. The grapevine that connected all the stewards in Cwmporth had swiftly sped the news to its stunned participants and, several stewards, in whose clubs Thomas had been used to spending some of his time off, came to see David and Pat. They offered their sympathies and reminded David that they would help him out in any way; he had only to ask. And then they went away, leaving David to grapple with the bar accounts and to ensure that the money from the No. 2 account was removed from the till reading.

Most of the club members also approached David and Pat to say how sorry there were about the news. The committee offered to close the club on Christmas Day as a mark of respect for Thomas. When the secretary, Alf Smith, conveyed the offer to David it became clear during the conversation between them that the committee had voted against the wishes of the chairman, who was for opening as usual. David politely declined and told the secretary that it was not what his father would have wanted and, in any event, he and his mother had decided that the best way to cope was to keep busy, especially on Christmas Day. The two men did agree, however, to close the club on the morning and afternoon of the funeral, and David informed the secretary that he would open the club at seven in the evening so that everyone could enjoy the Christmas Eve festivities.

Pat and David were about to leave to visit the chapel of rest at the top end of Coronation Road when there was a knock at the door. It was Mary O'Flaherty wanting to speak to Pat so David invited her into the front room, which had been cleaned and made ready for tomorrow's gathering of friends and relatives.

-It's not much at a time like this, said Mary with genuine feeling, but every little helps.

She handed Pat an unsealed envelope in which a small wad of pound notes was clearly visible.

-I went round the whole street and everyone chipped in. Mrs. Jones gave me notes for all the coins, explained Mary.

Pat held the envelope tightly and tried to prevent her hands from shaking.

-It's very kind of you. What can I say? You will thank everyone for me, won't you Mary?

-Of course. There was money too for some flowers but we've sent them to the undertakers.

-We were just going there now to see dad, said David.

Thomas's false teeth had been restored to their rightful place and David and Pat both agreed that he didn't look half bad at all. In fact, said Pat, they'd done a good job so that his face looked quite natural, like he was asleep or resting with his eyes closed. She smoothed the hair at the side of her husband's temples and the tears from her eyes rolled down her face and fell softly to the subdued carpet. Her body felt physically pierced by the awful loneliness and her bewildered mind was tortured by the thought of the empty bed that would always await her; the future seemed to hold no more for her now than days full of tears and nights alone in a cold bed. Pat held out her hand for David to take it in his and together they gazed upon Thomas's tranquil face from which all traces of his death agony had been removed.

-I'm glad I came to see him. But I shall remember him as he was, not as he is now, said Pat.

On their way out, they met the undertaker and gave him some items to go in the coffin and then arm in arm they left and emerged into the cold December light.

Pat never again went to see her husband but that evening when the club was still not too busy and the new barmaid felt she was able to cope, David found twenty minutes to return to the funeral parlour. He had to wait for a few moments in a small reception area while the undertaker moved Thomas's body from the refrigerator to the chapel, but soon father and son were alone in the sombre, soft-carpeted room. Thomas looked splendid, and David was cheered that he would be able to tell his mother that the items they had left had all been arranged as they had instructed. Inside the casket by Thomas's right side was a small bottle of beer, while around his neck was a Brigade of Guards tie, a Christmas present from David. The blue and dark red stripes of the tie stood out sharply against the white shirt, and on his left breast above his heart was the regimental crest of the Welsh Guards, which Pat had bought to complement the tie.

David gazed sadly at his father's body through the tears that started to well up in his eyes. Thomas's tall frame seemed to fit the coffin with a natural but chilling simplicity. Duw, he wouldn't have liked the make-up on his face, thought David. Now that no answer would ever come, there were so many questions that David still wanted to ask his father; so many things he wanted to know. He began to talk to Thomas in a soft voice, to reassure him that matters were in hand at the club; that the committee had actually mustered enough balls to go against Charlie Hawkins; and that he was pretty sure he'd sorted out the No. 2 account business. And when the matter-of-fact had been taken care of and David's tears could no longer be contained, he wept bitterly and cradled his father's hand in his own. The cold, pitiless, feel of the bony hand almost made David recoil in horror for there was no warmth there, only sharp, bent fingers and the starkness of death. Between his sobs, David told his father how much he missed him and how he loved him still. Although his father would never have doubted it, he promised to look after his mother and to live up to his father's example as best he might. Tomorrow, they would bury him and David knew that it was time to say farewell. Gently he moved the position of the tie so that it fell in proper Guardsman-like fashion in a straight line along the shirt front, and then David kissed his father's brow and never again did he look upon the face of Thomas Rhys.

The funeral went off as well as could be expected and Thomas's few surviving close relatives all turned up and gave their support. A large crowd, mostly of women who traditionally did not attend the burial at the cemetery, stood silently along the length of Granall Street as the funeral cortege set off towards the chapel of rest. Thomas's coffin was surrounded by flowers as the big black car, which comes eventually to collect us all, drove slowly to the end of the street. Neither Pat nor David had told the undertaker that Thomas had been raised as a Presbyterian so the service at the chapel of rest was conducted by a Church of England vicar - for when in doubt everyone resorts to them. It didn't matter, however, for Thomas's Welsh chapel days were long behind him and he, at least, wouldn't have cared tuppence if a witch doctor had led the singing. Mind, the singing was good; in fact, with so many people there from the valleys - friends and former miners - the hymns acquired an emotional edge that the vicar and the undertaker rarely witnessed in the course of carrying out their duties in the relatively anglicised Cwmporth. When the brief service was over and the lilting strains of Welsh voices echoed no more, the women - including Pat - went back to the house to see to the food and drink, while the men went on to the cemetery.

The cold wind, which threatened to bring a heavy snowfall, whipped across the hillside where the large crowd was gathered to lay Thomas Rhys in the stony ground. Many of the men pulled their coat collars about their necks and stood unflinchingly around the open grave. David watched impassively, his head bowed to catch a final glimpse of the nameplate on the lid, as the coffin was lowered and the last words were said over his father's body. In a few minutes the ceremony was over; a good number of mourners came upto David to say kind words about his father, which he accepted warmly, and then people began to file away. They would soon pick up the threads of Christmas that for the funeral they had set aside briefly. The driver of a funereal car held open the door for David who, for a moment, hesitated. Nearly all the crowd had left and David turned slowly to look back at the grave next to which two men with shovels were waiting patiently. Yes, he thought, soon they'll cover him over and eventually the black dust in his lungs will mingle with the dust of his body. The thought was almost more than David could bear and he quickly got into the car and the driver shut the door tightly behind him.

The rest of the day was fully occupied in being hospitable to those who packed the Rhys's front room. When they had all departed, Pat was persuaded to take another sedative and then she was put to bed so that she could sleep and block out the pain. At seven o'clock David opened the club and there was soon a steady stream of customers to keep him and the barmaid busy. The concert evening had been cancelled and people were content just to sit and drink among friends. Many of the members told David that he had lost a good man in his father and wished their condolences to be passed to his mother. Invariably, these brief encounters proved to be somewhat awkward for it is difficult to commiserate with someone when surrounded by so many people having an enjoyable time. It was only natural that the beer consumed would loosen tongues, which had at the start of the evening been unnaturally quiet in recognition of David's loss; and it was equally to be expected that friends gathered together around the tables in the club would not for long be able to resist the exchange of smiles and then the onset of laughter. So, it was not a lack of respect or a cruel disregard for David's feelings that led to the lively conviviality, it was simply that the combination of alcohol and friendship made such an outcome inevitable. For David the club appeared exactly the same - full of swirling smoke, the clink of glasses, and the telling of tales. Nothing had changed, except that there had been no sign at all that evening of

Charlie Hawkins. It was almost as if his father had never lived, and had never died underneath the spot where David was standing now. When it came to stop tap, which the committee had stipulated would be at ten thirty, all the members were very good about drinking up without delay and several of them helped David to return the glasses to the bar where the barmaid washed them and put them away in quick time. No one hung on for an after-hours drink and, most unusually, David was able to lock up just before eleven o'clock.

The fire had gone out and it felt cold and dank when David entered the scullery. The whole house was still and silent and for a moment David was frightened. He rushed upstairs and to his relief he found his mother asleep in the bedroom. David spread an extra blanket over her and then returned downstairs. Quietly, so as not to awake and alarm his mother, he slipped out through the front door and headed towards the river.

David leaned against the rusted rail at the side of the jetty and looked down into the grey water. The tide was high and strong and running now back towards the sea. It had started to snow and, in the dim light, David saw the flakes fall into the swirling current and disappear. In the power station nearby someone had tripped a switch and the Rush sprang into life; it bubbled and hissed below David as its waters were churned out to join again the flow of the Effyl. A thin white coating of snow covered the wooden floor of the jetty and some flakes clung to David's hair. David moved away from the rail and looked out over the broad river. The remains of the Sceptre Works were silhouetted against the low angry clouds. The support pylons of the jetty swayed slightly and silently under the pounding of the Rush, which caused David to cast his gaze upon the turmoil below. He became mesmerised by the popping and twisting flux of the Rush so that he remained motionless, staring into the river, for some while.

The sound of a ship's siren barrelling along the channel of the river from its source further downstream snapped the river's hold on David.

It was Christmas Day. He knew that in churches throughout the land the worthless prayers of thousands attending midnight mass would be seeping through the walls and ceilings and reaching up into an uncomprehending sky whose only response was the soft tumbling snow. The flakes were falling now on the deserted steelworks and on the hopeless streets throughout Riverside. The delicate patterns of those dropping into the Effyl were instantly destroyed. Further north, among the valleys and the hills, the snow had thickened and it was falling heavily on the remains of Ty-Triste. It fell too on a hillside in Cwmporth onto a fresh grave. Pat Rhys, who had been able to sleep only fitfully, was now awake - surrounded by her peeling wallpaper - and was thinking how cold it must be inside that grave.

David left the jetty and walked towards Granall Street. The snow muffled everything and disguised the ugliness around him, but even the white shroud that descended now over Riverside could not hide from David his own despair.

About the Author

Mike Stephens was born in 1951 into a mining family in Tredegar but grew up in Newport, south Wales. At various times, he has worked as a bus conductor, airport worker, power station operative, and as a dolomite in a steel factory. Mostly, however, he has long been employed as a university academic, specialising in the fields of policing and criminal justice. When not working, he has travelled extensively in the far east and Africa, especially Namibia and Botswana. He supports Welsh rugby and Tottenham, and spends a great deal of his time watching cricket.